GRENI LABYRINTH

A John Decker Novel

ANTHONY M.STRONG

WEST
STREET

ALSO BY ANTHONY M. STRONG

THE JOHN DECKER SUPERNATURAL THRILLER SERIES

Soul Catcher (prequel) • What Vengeance Comes • Cold Sanctuary

Crimson Deep • Grendel's Labyrinth • Whitechapel Rising

Black Tide • Ghost Canyon • Cryptic Quest • Last Resort

Dark Force • A Ghost of Christmas Past • Deadly Crossing

Final Destiny

THE REMNANTS SERIES

The Remnants of Yesterday • The Silence of Tomorrow

STANDALONE BOOKS

The Haunting of Willow House • Crow Song

AS A.M. STRONG WITH SONYA SARGENT

Patterson Blake FBI Mystery Series

Never Lie To Me • Sister Where Are You • Is She Really Gone

All The Dead Girls • Never Let Her Go • Dark Road From Sunset

GRENDEL'S LABYRINTH

West Street Publishing

This is a work of fiction. Characters, names, places, and events are products of the author's imagination. Any similarity to events or places, or real persons, living or dead, is purely coincidental.

Cover art and interior design by Bad Dog Media, LLC.

ISBN: 9781942207115

CLASSIFIED UNIVERSAL SPECIAL PROJECTS

VERUM CONQUISITOR

For Sonya—who scares easily

PROLOGUE

IRELAND – 1495 A.D.

BROTHER DEAGLÁN Ó Coileáin laid down his bible on the small wooden desk, pushed his stool back, and stood up. Having spent the last several hours in silent prayer, he now felt the first flutters of uncertainty for the duty which lay ahead.

He crossed to the window, looked out over the darkened evening landscape, toward the barely perceptible flickers of yellow light that marked the distant village. It was the tithes from this small community that kept the monastery in operation. If the villagers only knew the true purpose of the holy building, and the evil it guarded, they might rethink their decision to live in such close proximity.

Brother Deaglán sighed.

The time was drawing close.

As if to underscore this awareness of the approaching hour, a light knock interrupted his introspection.

Deaglán turned toward his cell door but said nothing in response. He hadn't spoken a word for twelve years, since joining the order as a fourteen-year-old boy and taking a vow of silence. Even so, he made his way to the door, touching the treasured bible one last time on the way out. Two monks stood in the corridor, older men who had been instrumental in his spiritual training. Now they waited for him to join them on one last journey, their hands clasped together, lips moving in silent devotion.

Deaglán allowed himself to be led along dim passageways. They moved single file, one monk ahead of him, and one behind, until they reached the monastery's nave. Here in this holy place, candles burned, casting pools of yellow light into the frigid air and throwing long shadows. This was not, however, Deaglán's ultimate destination. They continued on, through the south transept, and down a set of narrow stone steps that wound into the underbelly of the building.

The crypt was noticeably colder than the nave, surrounded as it was by thick windowless stone walls that held back the frozen earth beyond. The air was stale, as if it had been trapped here for an eternity. Deaglán wondered if it was the proximity to what lay ahead that tainted the atmosphere so. This place was the opposite of all that went above. It was unholy. Godless. A chamber older than anyone could recall, over which the monastery's stones and timbers had been placed. This was, he thought, the last place on earth anyone should ever be. His mere presence felt blasphemous.

They moved through the crypt, and under an archway, into a second, larger room. Here a clutch of his brethren stood motionless, their features transformed into ghastly caricatures by the flickering light from torches placed in notches along the walls.

They watched as he entered, and in their eyes, Deaglán sensed a deep sadness—and something else. Fear.

The abbot, a sickly thin man with graying wisps of wiry hair clinging to his scalp, nodded a somber greeting. He broke from the monks and proffered a flaming torch.

Deaglán nodded a grim acknowledgment and accepted the offering, the sudden heat a welcome respite from the biting chill.

In front of him stood a door of sturdy oak secured with a

mighty iron bolt. Intricate carvings had been cut into the wood, demons that clawed their way up from a rendition of hell that he recognized from the darker passages of his bible.

As Deaglán approached, the monks parted to allow him passage. At the door he paused. His previous trepidation now flared into a writhing terror. This was the moment he had been preparing for since he entered the monastery. Over those many years he had witnessed others, those that came before him, linger in this exact spot. He had stood voiceless as they stepped through this very door.

And he had listened to their dying screams.

Now, as he gathered the will to keep going, Deaglán found that his faith was not the comfort he hoped it would be. But it was too late now, he must honor his commitment. Deaglán drew back the bolt. The door creaked inward. He glanced back, at the gathered monks, then proceeded into the darkness beyond.

Behind him, the door slammed shut. A scrape of metal on metal indicated the securing of the bolt, and the finality of his situation.

The torch flickered.

Deaglán squinted into the gloom and found himself in a tight vaulted corridor with walls lined in stone. Up ahead was another door, this one hardly ornate, made of roughhewn planks. A thick beam slotted into brackets in the frame held this one more securely than the first.

Deaglán approached the inner door. He could feel his heart thudding in his chest. Blood roared in his ears. Now he faltered. What horrors waited on the other side of this portal?

But there was no turning back. The outer door was already locked, and the monks on the other side, the same people he had broken bread with for so many years, would never allow him to return. This was too important. More so than one lonely life. So Deaglán gathered his courage, said a last prayer, that his death would be quick, and heaved the beam aside.

The darkness beyond the second door was absolute. The

ANTHONY M. STRONG

torch barely made a dent in the blackness, but Deaglán could tell that the walls were now rough stone. Gone were the smooth blocks that lined the crypt and flagstones that paved the ground. This was a cave. More than that, it was a labyrinth.

Deaglán's hand shook. The torch flame leaped and danced, flickering on a chill breeze. Then, before Deaglán could protect it, a swift gust snatched the light away.

The torch blew out.

Deaglán was drenched in absolute blackness. He stopped, fighting the urge to flee back to the locked and impassable door. His breath came in ragged, terrified gasps.

From somewhere ahead, a grunt, low and menacing.

Deaglán dropped the useless torch, put his hands together and kneeled on the soft earthen floor. He turned his face upward to heaven and begged the Lord to deliver him from his fear.

Another grunt, louder this time, came accompanied by a blast of fetid, foul air.

Deaglán retched on the carrion stench. He could feel his hands trembling in the dark, even though he could not see them.

Something brushed against his face, a light touch that moved across his cheek and lingered on his neck. It felt like... a fingernail, long and sharp.

Deaglán recoiled, his skin crawling.

Hot, rancid breath wafted toward him.

Whatever he shared this chamber with was close. Inches from his face. He could sense it. He also knew that even though he was blind, the creature that stood before him was not. It could see him as if it was daylight. Worse, it was relishing his terror, lapping it up the way a deer drank at a cool stream.

Deaglán's mind snapped.

He forgot about prayers to a god he knew had abandoned him. He didn't care about the monks that were depending on him to fulfill his duty. All Deaglán wanted in that moment, was to escape the fiend that circled him, feeding on his fear. But there was nowhere to go, because he could not see, and a sturdy door

4

carved with the likeness of demons blocked his only escape route. So instead he coiled into a ball and began to cry. And then, as unseen hands lifted him from the floor, and unseen jaws ripped into his trembling flesh, Deaglán broke his vow of silence for the first time since entering the monastery and screamed.

ONE

OFF THE COAST OF NEW ENGLAND—PRESENT DAY

THE LATE MORNING sun glinted off the Gulfstream jet's sleek fuselage as the aircraft flew northeast following the New England coast. Below them, a blanket of silky white clouds stretched beyond the horizon. Soon, the jet would cross into Canada and Newfoundland, where they would turn further east and onward toward their destination. Dublin, Ireland.

Decker had left Nancy at the hotel hours earlier and taken a cab to the executive airport. He'd been reticent to leave her behind in Florida, but his old friend, Bill Gibson, had promised to be there should she need him. Besides, there was still a week of their vacation left, and Decker didn't want her to miss out on that. She would, he knew, fill her days with trips to the beach and hours in the hotel spa, activities Decker had little interest in.

Upon arriving at the airport, a pair of burly men in black suits and dark sunglasses met Decker. With stiff professionalism that reminded him of the Secret Service operatives with whom he had crossed paths once or twice during his stint as a New York detective, they escorted him to a private hanger on the far side of the airfield. Here a plain white unmarked Gulfstream G550 sat fueled up and waiting.

So was Adam Hunt.

He stood at the bottom of the air stairs with his arms folded. If he was pleased to see Decker, he did not show it but merely turned and ascended the stairs without waiting to see if Decker would follow him up.

As they entered the plane, Decker tapped his new employer on the shoulder. "You said a travel bag would be packed for me. I don't see one."

"I took the liberty of purchasing all you would need," Adam replied without turning around. "Have no fear. Your bag is stowed already. I think you will find the selection of clothes to be more than satisfactory."

"You don't even know my size," Decker replied.

"If anything doesn't fit, feel free to purchase more clothing after we arrive in Ireland." Hunt stopped now and turned back to Decker. He held out a passport. "You'll need this."

Decker took it, noting the date of issue just a few days prior. "You thought of everything."

"Indeed." Hunt resumed his entry onto the aircraft. "Shall we take our seats? The cabin crew will not serve coffee until we are at cruising altitude. Therefore, I intend to be at cruising altitude as swiftly as possible."

Now, hours later, Decker relaxed in the jet's luxurious cabin, sitting in a white leather seat more sumptuous than any airplane seat he'd ever occupied. Facing him in another similarly well-appointed seat, Adam Hunt reclined with his eyes closed, hands placed neatly in his lap, as if he was sleeping. But he was not.

"Rory," Adam said to the occupant of a seat across the aisle. "Now that we are well and truly underway, why don't you fill Mr. Decker in regarding our little jaunt."

"Right you are." Rory McCormick was a diminutive man in his late thirties, barely five feet tall, with a crop of shaggy straw-blonde hair. He had been introduced as the expedition's archeologist, a role Decker found intriguing but upon which Hunt initially refused to elaborate. Now he leaned forward, eyes sparkling with scholarly excitement. "Have you ever heard of the Anglo-Saxon poem Beowulf?"

"Sure." Decker nodded. "Wasn't it something about an ancient warrior slaying an ogre?"

"A clumsy description," Rory said with a wry smile. "The poem tells the story of our titular hero, Beowulf, who comes to the aid of the Danish king, Hrothgar. After a mighty battle, he slays the beast, Grendel, a disfigured and terrifying creature that has been devouring the king's men while they sleep in the great hall. He then kills Grendel's mother by cutting off her head."

"A nice story," Decker said. "But I don't see what any of this has to do with us going to Ireland."

"Listen up, and you might find out," Adam said, his eyes still closed.

"Exactly." Rory licked his lips and removed an invisible speck of lint from his jacket. "There's only one copy of the poem known to exist–a manuscript known as the Nowell Codex. But here's where it gets interesting. Several years ago, NYPD confiscated a batch of ancient writings during the bust of an international antiquity smuggling operation in New York. Those documents contained an even older, more complete telling of the Beowulf story. In this version, the hero kills Grendel, and then the Danes, fearing him even in death, transport the body across the sea to Ireland. Here they bury him in an unmarked grave, far from the shores of Denmark."

"Ah." Decker nodded. "But it still doesn't explain why I'm sitting on this plane. It is still a story, even if you found an alternative ending."

"Actually, it's not. At least, not entirely." Hunt opened his eyes now. He raised the seat into its upright position and cleared his throat. "There are scholars who believe that the poem draws on real history, and historical figures, in its narrative. King Hrothgar for example, is probably based upon a genuine Danish king. Excavations of burial mounds in Uppsala, Sweden, have turned up evidence supporting the existence of other characters from the text. They even found the remains of a sixth-century hall in the exact location where Hrothgar's mead hall was supposed to be. Other texts and poems from the time also mention the hall, adding to the likelihood of its reality."

"You aren't seriously saying that Beowulf and Grendel were real, are you?" Decker raised an eyebrow.

"Why not?" Hunt replied. "You of all people should be open to the possibility of such things."

"I am," Decker said. "But even if they were real, both Beowulf and Grendel are long dead."

"They are." Hunt nodded. "But that doesn't mean we aren't interested in them."

"Or more precisely, Grendel," Rory added. "The older manuscript mentioned the Danes burying Grendel in Ireland, but it provided scant clues regarding exactly where."

"Which is why we've been funding Archeological digs across the entire country for the past fourteen years, in the hopes that one of them would turn something up," Hunt said.

"And now it has." Rory was grinning from ear to ear. "A team excavating the remains of an eleventh-century monastery made an exciting find a few days ago. If what they discovered turns out to be the real deal..."

"We'll have proved that the tale of Beowulf is not a story at all," Hunt interjected. "But a historical document."

"What did they find?" Decker's curiosity was piqued, despite his lack of interest in the hoarier elements of the tale.

"Grendel," Rory said, the excitement in his voice palpable. "We think we've found Grendel, or more accurately, his bones."

TWO

FATHER PATRICK CLEARY left his home in the village of Clareconnell, and made his way along Winslow Road, past the church where he said Mass every day of the week and twice on Sundays. He nodded a greeting to Sean O'Mara–erstwhile farmer turned village odd job man–who was hurrying toward the Claddagh Arms and continued toward a lonely cottage on the edge of town. It was late in the evening, a little after nine, and the summer sun was slipping low on the horizon. Father Cleary would rather have been partaking of the crumpets and cup of hot tea his housekeeper brought him every night and which would, by now, be growing cold on the side table in his living room. But when duty called, Father Cleary answered, regardless of circumstance, or the proximity to supper time.

Now, as he approached his destination, a whitewashed brick building with a slate roof, he prepared himself for the spiritual task that lay ahead. In one hand he clutched a satchel containing the holy oils, bible, and the Eucharist–to be administered only after the parishioner he was attending had made full and final penance for his sins.

He entered the cottage and climbed the stairs to a back bedroom.

11

Tom Walsh lay fevered and pale in a narrow iron-framed bed, a duvet covering the elderly man's wasted frame, despite the warm weather that rendered the cottage's interior oppressive and hot.

"I'll need room here to administer the last rites," Father Cleary said to the gathered family that crowded into the small space. Molly Walsh, her sister, Anne, and two grown sons, Brendan and Kieran. "Before Tom leaves us."

Mrs. Walsh ushered them out, into the hallway, then returned to the door and watched the priest. She was a plump woman with ruddy cheeks and a smile that never wavered. Tonight however, her demeanor was sad. Her tear-stained face was, Cleary thought, as much a picture of anguish as ever he had seen.

Turning toward the bed, Father Cleary opened his satchel and arranged its contents on the nightstand. That done, he leaned over and touched his fingers to the clammy, cold skin of the elderly man's forehead.

"Father?" Tom's voice was brittle, barely more than a croak.

"I'm here, Tom," Father Cleary said. "I'll be anointing you presently, but first you must make penance."

"Penance?" Tom coughed, the sound dry, rasping, as if he were already a corpse. "What's the point. I know where I'm going."

"You're going to heaven, Tom." Father Cleary took up the vial of holy oils. "We should continue, there isn't much time."

"I'm scared." Tom's eyes, once a brilliant blue, now were cloudy and gray as he looked up toward the priest. "I don't want this."

"No one does," Cleary replied. "But this day will come for us all, in time."

Tom nodded. He ran his tongue across dry, cracked lips and deposited a thin sheen of spittle that moistened them temporarily.

Father Cleary turned to the nightstand and took up the bible, ready to recite the litany of the saints, but when he turned back, Tom was no longer looking at him. Instead, Father Cleary found nothing but cold, dead eyes that stared toward the ceiling.

Behind him, in the doorway, he heard a choked sob.

Cleary glanced around to see Molly Walsh, her hands to her face, fresh tears upon her cheeks.

"He's gone then," she said, looking past the priest toward her deceased husband.

"I'm afraid he has," Cleary confirmed. "And he's all the better for it."

She made the sign of the cross, then went to her husband, leaned over, and kissed his forehead. Next, she walked to the mirror hanging near the window, took it down, and placed it on the floor facing the wall.

"So that his soul won't see how thin and pale he's become," she explained, then returned to the bed. "I'll have my boys make him decent and bring the body down to the parlor ready for the wake. Once Doctor Laurel has signed the death certificate, of course."

"We won't be doing that, Molly," Cleary replied, with all the sympathy he could muster. "There will be no wake."

"There's always a wake," Molly said, the sorrow on her face replaced with determination. "It's tradition."

"Not for Tom, I'm afraid." Father Cleary shook his head. "We'll hold the funeral in the morning. I'll be sending the undertakers first thing. You should say your goodbyes and have him ready by then."

"Just a few days," Molly pleaded. "That's all I'm asking."

"I'm sorry. It can't be done." Father Cleary took her hand in his. A gentle touch. "We haven't had a death in the village for almost a year. There isn't time."

THREE

AT 10 P.M. LOCAL TIME, the Gulfstream started its descent into Dublin. Decker had spent the previous three hours of the flight in a light, fitful sleep. After listening to the tale of Beowulf, and Rory's admission that they had discovered the grave site of Grendel—previously considered a purely mythical figure—he had pressed Adam Hunt for more information, but the stoic, tight-lipped operative refused to elaborate. Instead, he cited agency protocols on unnecessary disclosure of information. Having assured Decker that a more detailed briefing would follow in good time, Hunt took his leave and disappeared into a stateroom at the rear of the aircraft. He had remained there ever since. Rory, an apparent introvert, produced a thick volume on ancient Rome from his carry-on bag and studied it with no attempt to continue conversation. Lacking any entertainment of his own with which to pass the time, Decker looked out of the window and watched the featureless horizon slip by, drank a cup of tea provided by the equally terse cabin attendant, and then dozed as day turned to night.

Now, as the jet dropped altitude and circled for its final approach, Adam Hunt reappeared. Wordless, he took up his former position opposite Decker and buckled himself in.

The airport was quiet when they touched down, most of the day's scheduled flights having come or gone already. The pilot wasted no time in maneuvering them across the airfield to a hanger as secure as the one from which they had departed. There would be no arrivals lounge or baggage carousel for this flight, apparently. Instead, a lone customs official boarded the aircraft and conducted a cursory check of their papers, then left just as quickly.

Decker descended the air stairs to find a swanky new Land Rover Discovery waiting for them, complete with driver. Hunt gave the man a warm greeting, embracing him with an easy familiarity that Decker found surprising. Adam Hunt did not, if his limited past experience was anything to go by, possess a very effusive personality.

"This here is Colum O'Shea," Hunt said to Decker, his enthusiasm fading as quickly as it had manifested to be replaced by a more familiar unreadability. "He'll be our point man here in Ireland."

"Pleased to meet you," Decker shook Colum's hand.

"Right back at you." Colum's soft Irish accent stood in stark contrast to Hunt's stiff pronunciation. "As soon as the bags are in the boot, we'll be on our way. I'm sure you're all dog tired."

"I could use a soft bed," Decker admitted. He was still sore from his encounter in the Florida woodland days before and relished the thought of an easy first assignment in the rolling Irish countryside. Hunt had refused to fully elaborate but poking around an archeological excavation didn't sound particularly stressful. A bunch of old bones would be, Decker reflected, a welcome change from the situations he'd found himself in over the past year. Best of all, nothing would try to eat him.

The luggage had been removed from the aircraft now, and once packed into the Land Rover's copious trunk, they bundled into the vehicle and left the airport behind.

It was dark outside. They departed Dublin and were soon

following narrow roads into the country's heartland. No sooner had they left the city behind, than Hunt turned to Decker.

"I assume you brought your cell phone?" he asked.

"Yes," Decker replied. "I added an international plan before I left the hotel back in Florida, so that Nancy can get ahold of me if she needs to."

"Give it to me." Hunt held out his hand.

"What?" Decker asked. "Why?"

"It's traceable. Now that you work for us, you must be discreet."

Decker hesitated.

"Don't worry," Hunt said, a tinge of frustration in his voice. "You'll still be able to call Nancy if you wish."

"Fine." Decker grudgingly handed over the phone.

"That's better." Hunt made sure it was off and tucked it into the Land Rover's glove compartment. He offered Decker a different phone. "Take this. Works anywhere in the world, and it's secure. No one can eavesdrop or track our whereabouts."

"Seems a little paranoid," Decker said, accepting the phone.

"We're careful, that's all." Hunt smiled. "Calls from authorized contacts will be securely rerouted to your new phone."

"Authorized contacts?"

"Yes. Nancy. Taylor. Your friend, Bill Gibson," Hunt replied. "With the caveat that you must not reveal your location or any mission critical details."

"Nancy already knows where I am," Decker said. "I told her last night."

"I think we can overlook the breach of protocol this one time," Hunt said. "I brought you on this trip because it doesn't require a high level of secrecy. Most of your missions will not be so mundane."

"Breaking me in, huh?"

"Something like that." Hunt turned forward again. "Even so, you should press upon Nancy the need for discretion."

Decker nodded and studied the phone, then slipped it into

his pocket and settled down into the seat. They drove south for two hours, passing through small towns and villages. Conversation was light and sporadic. The five-hour time difference meant that it was only early evening back in Florida, but their dawn rendezvous and many hours in the air had left Decker exhausted, and he suspected that the others felt the same.

A little after midnight they arrived at their destination. The village of Clareconnell was tiny, comprising a clutch of stone cottages with slate roofs, a church, and a scattering of surrounding farms. Their accommodation, a pub called The Claddagh Arms, occupied a central location on Winslow Road, the village's main thoroughfare.

The bar itself was closed for the night, last call having passed an hour since, but the landlord, brimming with Irish hospitality, offered to reopen so they could enjoy a nightcap. When they declined, he led them to their rooms on the pub's second floor. Minutes later, after freshening up, Decker crawled into bed. A more complete exploration of the luggage Hunt had provided him could wait until tomorrow. All Decker wanted to do was sleep.

FOUR

DECKER WAS the last to arrive at breakfast. When he entered the pub's barroom, which also doubled as a dining room for the accommodations above, he found his three companions huddled over a table in the back corner.

"Sleep well?" Hunt looked up as Decker approached and sat down.

"Like a log," Decker replied.

"I see the clothes we purchased are a good fit." Hunt eyed Decker's outfit, a white polo shirt and a pair of multi-pocketed tan cargo pants.

"I look like I'm off for a day of fly-fishing," Decker grumbled. "Not really my style."

"You look just fine. My people did a good job, as always."

"They thought of everything, I'll give them that," Decker said. "There's even a woolen sweater and a raincoat."

"This is Ireland." Hunt chuckled. "Just because its summer doesn't mean you won't need those."

"I guess so." Decker looked up as the waiter arrived, who also happened to be the landlord they had met the previous evening. He ordered a coffee and picked up the menu. "I don't suppose you serve grits?"

18

The landlord shook his head. "I'm afraid our offerings don't run to the exotic, but I might be able to rustle up a bowl of porridge. Oatmeal, as you Americans call it."

Before Decker could answer, Hunt interjected.

"He'll have the full Irish breakfast."

"I will?"

"You will," Hunt replied. "Trust me, you'll like it."

The landlord retreated toward a door next to the bar, no doubt the kitchen. Decker glanced around, noted that they were the room's only occupants. "It's quiet in here. I guess this place doesn't get a lot of overnight guests."

"We're the only ones." Hunt sipped his coffee. "Except for Robert and Astrid."

"And they are?" Decker asked.

"The team that made the discovery," Rory said.

"The archaeologists."

"Yes." Rory nodded. "I can't wait to get up to the site and see what they found. This is exciting."

"They should be here soon," Hunt said. "We agreed to meet for breakfast before heading out to the dig."

"Well, they'd better hurry," Colum said, as the food arrived. "Or I might just eat everything before they get here. This looks delicious."

Decker examined his own plate, loaded with rashers of thick cut bacon, bangers, mushrooms, eggs, and baked beans. He found the latter odd. Beans for breakfast? But what confounded him the most were the two unidentified discs that looked like sliced sausage. He prodded at them with his fork.

"Those are white and black puddings," Colum said. "They're fantastic. You'll love them."

"Okay." Decker was not convinced. "But what are they, exactly?"

"The lighter one is made of oatmeal, fat, and pork liver," Hunt said between mouthfuls. "The darker one is the same thing, but with pig's blood in it."

"Come again?" Decker's appetite was waning.

"You're not put off by a little blood, are you?" Hunt asked, amused. "Aren't you from Louisiana, where they eat alligators and frog's legs?"

"Sure," Decker admitted. "I've eaten some alligator in my time, but this is too much."

"I'll eat them if you're not going to." Colum reached across the table and skewered the puddings with his fork. "Waste not, want not. That's what my old man always said."

"Have at it." Decker turned his attention to the rest of the meal. Once he tucked in, it wasn't all that bad. The sausages were mild, nowhere near like the spicy links back home, but they had a certain appeal. The bacon reminded him of a ham steak. His hunger returned. He polished off the plate in a matter of minutes. Even the beans.

"How was it, then?" Colum asked.

"Not bad," Decker admitted, soaking up the last of the egg yolk with a slice of buttered toast. "I could get used to it."

"We have a convert to the delights of a hearty breakfast." Colum grinned. "It'll set you up for the day, to be sure."

"No doubt." Decker craned his neck toward the stairs leading up to the guest rooms, then turned to Hunt. "Shouldn't your people be here by now?"

"I would have expected as much." Hunt glanced at his watch. "It's getting late."

"Maybe they forgot about us and went straight up to the dig?" Colum offered.

"Unlikely." Hunt motioned to the landlord. "Harry, a word in your ear."

"Yes, sir." Harry dropped the towel with which he was wiping down the bar top in slow, lazy circles, and hurried over to the table. "How can I help you?"

"There are two guests staying upstairs. A man and a woman," Hunt said. "Robert McCray and Astrid Hansen."

"That's right." Harry nodded.

"They were supposed to meet us here, but they haven't shown up. You haven't seen them this morning, have you?"

"well, now, I can't say that I have," Harry replied. "Nor last night either, which is unusual. They've been in the bar drinking every evening since they arrived in the village three weeks ago. Not the chattiest of folk, kept to themselves for the most part, but nice enough."

"So, the last time you saw them was…"

"Yesterday morning at breakfast. Grabbed a quick bite and then they were off to the old monastery right at the crack of dawn. They said there had been a breakthrough. They were quite excited."

"I see." Hunt wiped his mouth with a napkin and stood up. "I don't suppose you could tell us their room numbers?"

"I can do better than that." Harry motioned for them to fall in behind him. "I'll show you."

FIVE

DECKER and the others followed Harry up to the second floor and past their own rooms to a pair of doors at the far end of the corridor.

"Here we are," Harry said. "Astrid's in Room two. Robert's in three."

Hunt took the lead and knocked on the closer of the doors. "Astrid?"

There was no answer.

He knocked again. "Astrid, it's Adam Hunt."

"I don't think she's in there," Colum said.

"Clearly." Hunt moved on to the other door with the same result. He turned to Harry. "You have keys for these rooms?"

"Naturally." Harry nodded. "I'm not sure it'd be right to let you in though. Privacy and all that."

"It will be fine, I assure you. We need to find out where Astrid and Robert are, and if they came back from the dig yesterday evening."

"Well, alright." Harry didn't look pleased, but he fished a ring of keys out of his pocket, anyway. He flicked through them until he came to the ones he wanted and swiftly unlocked the doors. "Make it quick, will you? I'm off to fetch fresh towels from the laundry room. By the time I get back I'll expect you to be done."

"Thank you." Hunt watched the landlord retreat, then addressed Colum and Rory. "The pair of you check Robert's room. Mr. Decker and I will take Astrid's."

Rory nodded and stepped off into room three with Colum at his heels. Decker followed Hunt into Astrid's accommodations.

The room was cramped, just like Decker's own accomodation along the corridor. A single nightstand and wardrobe were the chamber's only furniture, except for a twin bed, neatly made with the covers pulled up and pillows fluffed.

"Looks like she didn't sleep here last night," Decker observed.

"All her clothes are present," Hunt noted, opening the slender wardrobe and riffling through several outfits on wire hangers. He glanced around, studying the room. "I don't see any sign that she returned from the dig site yesterday."

"Which means she must still be up there," Decker surmised. "I bet we find that her partner didn't return either."

"Possibly." Hunt went to the door and stepped back out into the corridor where Colum and Rory waited to confirm as much.

"Is it likely they would stay at the dig overnight?" Decker asked, joining the rest of the group.

"No." Hunt shook his head. "The monastery is nothing more than a ruin with little shelter from the elements, and the team doesn't have the equipment or supplies to live on site. Given the proximity of the village, we deemed it pointless."

"Surely they have a phone," Decker said.

"They do, and I've already called it," Colum replied. "There isn't service out at the monastery, but if they were anywhere in the village, it would have rung. It went to voicemail."

"It was worth a try," Hunt said.

"Since they are not here, and are not answering their phone,

I'm starting to fear the worst," Colum said. He was already pulling the car keys from his pocket. "I'll bring the Land Rover around front. We should go up there and find them."

"Agreed," Hunt said with a frown. "I have a bad feeling about this."

SIX

THEY HURRIED downstairs and through the empty bar, then waited for Colum to bring the Land Rover around to the front of the building. When it arrived, they piled in, with Hunt taking the front passenger seat while Decker and Rory climbed into the back.

It was dark when they had arrived the night before, and Decker had been tired, going straight to bed without a care for his surroundings. Now, as they drove along the main street, he got his first good look at the village. There was a clutch of shops. A greengrocer, butcher, and a small supermarket. There was a gas station with a single pump. A fish and chip shop that proclaimed the best *curry sauce and chips* in town, even though it was the village's only establishment serving such fare. Another sign in the same window, faded by the sun, advertised Donor Kebabs. Past the shops were rows of whitewashed stone cottages with brightly painted doors. A few, Decker noted, still had thatched roofs. A church dominated the east end of town, its medieval tower topped by an Irish flag whipping in the breeze. Outside of this, gathered on the sidewalk near a set of gates that opened into the church grounds, were a cluster of black-clad villagers. They congregated near a sleek black automobile with a hatch open at the rear.

A hearse.

Decker turned to watch as the Land Rover slowed and crawled past. A mark of respect. Pallbearers in stiff black suits hoisted the coffin onto their shoulders and moved off toward the church. A woman with wiry white hair, flanked by two younger men, followed behind, faces cloaked in solemn anguish. Behind these, the rest of the mourners fell into line and processed through the gates. Then the car was speeding up again and soon the village was behind them.

"The monastery isn't far out of town," Colum said as they weaved along country lanes so narrow that Decker flinched more than once as hedgerows crowded the sides of the vehicle. "We'll be there in ten minutes, tops."

"Have you been here before then?" Decker asked. "You seem to know your way around."

"I've driven down from Dublin twice over the past few weeks," Colum replied. "Just for the day."

Hunt glanced back at Decker between the seats. "It pays to keep an eye on our money. We've made a considerable investment in projects such as this over the years, and we've found that without close supervision people get lax."

"Which is why we would have noticed the team missing even if we hadn't come to the village," Colum said. "They are due to submit their weekly report by tomorrow evening."

"I see." Decker wondered how many operatives his new employer had around the world, and how many pies they had their fingers in. This new job got more intriguing by the moment.

"Look." Rory pointed excitedly. "There's the monastery."

Decker followed Rory's gaze and saw a crumbling stone building rising over the gently sloping fields. It was nothing more than a ruin, roofless, with partially collapsed walls and glassless windows. Decker could tell it must have been impressive in its day. And large. As they drew closer, he saw more ruins. The monastery's footprint took up a space larger than a football field. At one end a mostly preserved wall stood complete with an ornate round window that must have been spectacular before its panes had succumbed to the ages.

"That's the Rose Window," Rory said, correctly guessing what had drawn Decker's attention. "There would have been intricately crafted stained glass between the stonework. See how the edifice is situated to the east? The morning sun would stream in and fill the nave with a blaze of color. A reminder of God's majesty. Another smaller window to the west would have served the same purpose later in the day."

"That's enough, Rory," Hunt said as they turned through an open farm gate and onto a trail leading through the fields. "You can give John a history lesson in the bar tonight. At this moment we have more pressing concerns."

"Right, you are." Rory looked sheepish. He peered out of the window. "Look. There's a car parked up ahead near the ruins."

"That settles it," Colum said as they drew close. "They never left here last night."

"Question is, why?" Hunt frowned.

"Only one way to find out." Colum pulled up next to the car and stopped. "We find them and ask."

"Excellent idea," Hunt was already exiting the vehicle.

Colum got out and went to the other car, a white VW Bora with a rental car barcode affixed to the side window. He placed a hand on the hood. "Engine's stone cold and there's dew on the bonnet. Definitely been here all night."

"Come along." Hunt took off toward the ruins with Colum and Rory close behind.

Decker paused a moment and took in the barren landscape. There was nothing but craggy untended fields rolling away in every direction, interspersed here and there with boulders that thrust up out of the ground as if they were trying to escape the soil that trapped them. If the archaeologists had spent the night up here, he hoped they had found adequate shelter.

He turned and hurried after the others, soon finding himself surrounded by thick stone walls. The archaeologists had erected a white tent under a towering archway that would once have led to a side chapel. A table containing artifacts pulled from the ground, some small, others larger, stood within. More objects, waiting to be examined, lay in crates. There were square trenches too, arranged in quilt-like patches throughout the nave and staked out according to a grid pattern, the top layer of soil removed to reveal the earth below. Trowels, shovels, and brushes lay nearby.

"They aren't here." Colum stood with his hands on his hips and scanned the roofless space. "I don't get it."

"They must be around," Hunt said. "I want a thorough search made of the entire site. We'll split up. If anyone finds anything, just holler."

"Right." Colum nodded. "I'll take the area behind the nave and check the grounds."

"Good idea." Hunt motioned to Decker and Rory. "The two of you search the north and south transepts. I'll look in what used to be the cloisters. Let's find them, people."

They headed off in different directions.

Decker hurried under a half-collapsed archway and was soon in what remained of the south transept. Here the walls were lower, most of the stonework missing. The remains of windows, their glass long since gone, notched the walls at regular intervals. The floor was mostly grass, but here and there a flagstone remained, poking through the loose soil. Moss clung to the walls in the shadier sections like a thin green carpet. But it was the gaping hole in the center of the room, surrounded by piles of earth and a pair of recently removed flagstones, that caught Decker's attention. He hurried toward it, saw that the hole was actually an entrance into what must have been a previously concealed lower level. A set of worn stone steps wound into abysmal darkness. He took out his phone, turned on the flashlight, and aimed it down into the hole. It did nothing but illuminate the first few steps before fading into the gloom.

From somewhere in another section of the ruins, he could hear one of his companions moving around. Further away, Hunt was calling the names of the two lost archaeologists in a faint hope that they would answer. He garnered no response.

Decker stepped away from the hole and cupped his hands to his mouth, then shouted as loud as possible to draw attention to his find. Moments later three figures appeared, running from different parts of the monastery. He waited until his companions drew close and then pointed out the unearthed subterranean staircase.

"Intriguing." Hunt stepped close to the edge and peered down into the chasm, then turned back to the rest of the group. "Given that Robert and Astrid don't appear to be anywhere else, I'd say it's a fair bet that they are down there, don't you think?"

SEVEN

FATHER CLEARY WATCHED the pallbearers carry the coffin from the hearse up the path to the church doors, and inside. Behind it, following along in solemn silence, many of the village's residents had shown up to pay their respects to Tom Walsh, a man who had worked hard, and drank harder. After fifty years during which he'd nary missed a night knocking back pints at the Claddagh Arms, Tom had become a much loved, if outspoken, Clareconnell fixture. Now, in death, he would become something more.

Father Cleary waited for the coffin to reach its destination at the foot of the altar steps, while the grieving family, friends, and parishioners, took their places in the pews.

Molly Walsh wiped tears from her eyes and gazed at the coffin as if she could not believe what was happening. Father Cleary felt a pang of sadness. Under normal circumstances, Molly would have been accorded the time to give her husband the sendoff he rightly deserved. Tom would have laid in the darkened parlor of their small cottage, curtains drawn save for one window which would have been cracked open to allow his soul to take flight. Friends and family would have spent days paying their respects and lifting a glass to the old man.

This had not happened.

Cleary could only hope that poor Tom's soul would find its way free now, because the alternative was too awful to contemplate. For Tom to be trapped in his body when it went below was more than the priest could bear to think about. Instead, he raised his hands to the heavens, a sign that the service was about to begin.

A silence fell upon the gathered congregation.

The priest cleared his throat and began. An hour from now the service would be over and Tom would be taken away to serve the village like those who had died before him. But first, it was time to say goodbye.

EIGHT

DECKER, Rory, and Adam Hunt waited while Colum hurried back through the ruins to fetch flashlights from a box stored in the same tent as the recently unearthed artifacts. He soon returned, handing one heavy-duty flashlight to Decker, and keeping the other for himself.

"I could only find two," he said. "But at least we'll be able to see down there."

"We'll go down one by one," Hunt said to Colum. "We don't know how stable those steps are."

"Right." Colum nodded. "I'll go first. If I get down in one piece, the rest of you can follow."

"Good idea." Hunt nodded.

Colum clicked on his flashlight and shone it ahead of him as he placed a tentative foot on the top step. "Feels solid enough," he said, then moved in further until only his head and shoulders were visible. Soon these too disappeared beneath the ground.

They waited.

Decker peered into the hole, watching the slowly descending flashlight beam bob around as Colum traversed the circular staircase into the bowels of the monastery.

After another minute passed, Colum's voice drifted up from

below. "The stairs are fine. Slippery in places, but structurally solid."

"Good job," Hunt called down to him. "Shine your light back up so we can see. We're coming down."

"I'll take the rear," Decker said. "Since I have the other flashlight."

One by one they stepped into the hole and made their way underground. The steps were slippery, just as Colum had warned, slick in places with ground water that trickled out of the surrounding blocks. They took it slow, since there were no railings and scant places to hold on to, but soon reached the bottom where Colum waited, a grin on his face.

"Just look at this place," he said, sweeping his light around the chamber after they were all down safely. "It's incredible."

"Wow." Rory looked around in awe. "It sure is."

"The crypt," Hunt said.

Decker swung his own flashlight around the space, which he estimated to be at least thirty feet long by fifteen feet wide. The walls, made of chiseled stone, were pockmarked with age. A flagstone floor smoothed by countless feet led to a wide decorated arch beyond which there was nothing but darkness.

Hunt was moving off toward the archway.

Crossing the inner chamber, they arrived at a door carved with figures that writhed up out of what looked to Decker like a rendition of hell.

"Demons," Colum said. He made the sign of the cross.

"Unbelievable. When Robert said they had found the burial site of Grendel, I had no idea it would be so impressive. The pictures he sent us don't do it justice." Rory was talking fast, his words breathless. "This chamber clearly predates the building above. Note how the blocks fit together, the rough tooling on the walls and floor. And that door... It's breathtaking. Just think how long it's been down here, waiting in the darkness. We might be the first people to cast our eyes upon it in five hundred years."

"Except for Robert and Astrid," Hunt said. He went to the door and gave it a push. It opened inward on protesting hinges.

"Look at this." Colum nodded toward a pair of corroded iron bolts attached to the door. He examined them, his fingers probing several dings in the metal where the rust had chipped away. "Looks like they were rusted tight. Someone hammered them free."

"I told them to wait for us before they ventured beyond the crypt," Hunt said. "Intellectual curiosity obviously got the better of them."

"I don't understand," Decker said. "When we were on the plane you said they'd discovered the burial site of Grendel."

"That's right." Hunt nodded.

"If they hadn't gone past this door, and you instructed them not to venture further, how would they know what lay beyond, let alone that it was Grendel's burial site?"

"Because of this." Rory stepped up to the door and pointed. "There's an inscription here, carved into the wood above the demons."

"It's barely legible." Decker squinted to read it. "I can't understand what it says."

"That's because it's written in ecclesiastical Latin." Rory smirked, as if he was bursting to show off his skills. He read off the words, his index finger following along with each syllable. *"Hic jacet Grendel. Ipsum periculum turbare tua."*

"Is that supposed to mean something to me?" Decker asked.

"No, but the English translation should," Hunt interjected. "It means, *Here lies Grendel. Disturb him at your peril.*"

NINE

PALLBEARER SEAN O'MARA stood with his hand resting on a plain wooden crate atop a silver gurney and watched the line of mourners file out of the church, followed at the rear by Father Cleary. When the last of them had exited and the church doors swung closed, Sean gave the gurney a push and wheeled it toward the coffin.

"This is the part I hate," Craig Hennessy said, joining him from one of the pews, where he had been waiting patiently.

They were the only two left in the church now, and it would be their task to move Tom Walsh, a chore neither man relished.

"I'll be glad when Father Cleary recruits some new blood for this job," Sean grumbled. "It's high time someone else took up the reins."

"You're not wrong there." Craig nodded in agreement. He'd only done this a few times over the years, but it was more than enough. "I'll say this though, I'm glad I'm the one delivering the body, not the one in that coffin. Poor Tom. He doesn't deserve this kind of sendoff."

"None of us do." Sean was already looking forward to a cold pint in the Claddagh as soon as they were done with their grisly task. "It'll happen to us all, soon enough."

"Not me." Craig lifted the coffin lid and looked down at Tom Walsh dressed in his best suit, face taut and sallow, frozen in the grimace of death. Craig hesitated a moment, steeling himself, then took hold of the dead man's feet. "I swear, I'm getting away from this feckin village. No matter what you say, this ain't right. I'll be out of here long before it's my turn. You wait and see."

"And where will you go?" Sean hooked his hands under the corpse's shoulders and lifted. Together they swung the body over and into the plain wooden box atop the gurney.

I'm off to Dublin." Craig dropped the lid back onto the now empty coffin and helped lift a second lid over the rough crate that now housed Tom. "The big city."

"You're all talk, Craig Hennessy." Sean turned the gurney and wheeled it past the altar to a door near the Lady Chapel. "You'll never leave Clareconnell and you know it. Dublin, my arse. You wouldn't last ten minutes in the city. Besides, Ellen would never agree to such a thing."

"She's my wife." Craig opened the door. Beyond was a windowless chamber with a set of steps that descended beneath the church. "She'll follow where I go."

"Try telling her that," Sean chuckled. "And you'll be living in a rented room above the Claddagh. She's not one to put up with foolishness."

"I'll tell you what's foolish." Craig maneuvered the gurney to the head of the stairs. "Carting Tom Walsh down these steps instead of burying him in a Christian manner, that's what."

"Quit yer grumbling and lift." Sean gripped the rim of the box. "The sooner we get Tom where he's going, the quicker we'll get to the pub."

"You'll get no complaints from me on that one." Craig lifted his end and stepped backwards onto the first stair. Together the men huffed and heaved the box down until they reached a subterranean room with whitewashed brick walls. A single light bulb hung from a bare wire, the glow bathing the space in soft yellow light. As the men entered, the light swayed in a draft that wafted down the stairs from the church above, causing shadows to leap across the walls.

Here was another gurney, similar in construction to the one above, except the metal was pitted and scraped, dark and tarnished with age. The wheels were bare, the rubber long since crumbled. The men hoisted the box atop and paused to catch their breath.

"That's the hard bit over with." Sean wiped a sheen of sweat from his brow and leaned on the box. "It'll be easy going from here."

"Hard bit?" Craig leaned against the wall and dabbed his face with a crumpled handkerchief. "Don't make me laugh. It's what we have to do at the end of that tunnel that's the hard bit."

Both men glanced toward an opening in the wall opposite the stairs, and the sloping shaft that fell away into darkness.

"Well, I'll not argue that one." Sean went to the opening and flicked a switch, activating a string of bulbs that ran the length of the tunnel. He turned back to the wooden box and patted the rough wood. "Let's get Tom down there."

They pressed on, Craig at the gurney's front and Sean at the rear. Soon after they passed through the opening, their progress slowed. The tunnel was narrow and claustrophobic, barely wide enough to push the gurney which bumped along on the uneven, cracked floor. It was also in a terrible state of repair, and the further they moved away from the church, the more dilapidated the tunnel became. To add to their misery, condensation dripped in a steady patter from the arched ceiling above their heads. It also got darker as they ventured deeper into the tunnel where several bulbs had burned out.

Regardless, they pushed Tom Walsh along for fifteen minutes, passing right under the village. On ground level, twenty or more feet up, would be Winslow Road, and then as they continued further, empty farmland. It was with great relief that they reached their destination. A metal door secured with a hefty padlock.

Craig removed a key from a chain around his neck and unhitched the padlock. He reached out to slide the latch back and open the door, but then he hesitated.

"What are you waiting for, an invitation from the queen of England?" Sean grumbled from the rear. "Open it up for Pete's sake, man. I want out of this place."

"Give me a minute, will you?" Craig's voice trembled. "I hate this part. It gives me the willies."

"I'll give you more than that if you don't get that feckin door open." Sean gave the gurney a sharp push, jolting it into Craig's rear.

"Ow. There's no need to get testy." Craig glared at his companion. "I don't get paid for this you know."

"Well, neither do I," Sean snapped back. The Claddagh would be open by now, chock full of villagers looking to raise a glass to its recently departed best customer. The longer Craig prevaricated, the longer he would have to wait to join them. And Sean was thirsty. More to the point, a couple of beers would dull the memory of what he was about to do, and he wanted to be firmly on the other side of this particular task, glass in hand. "For the love of God, just open it."

"You're a grumpy sod, Sean O'Mara." Craig scowled, but he drew back the latch anyway, and pushed the door wide.

A blast of fetid, rotten air wafted from the room beyond.

Craig gagged and turned away, covering his mouth. He hit the lid of the box containing Tom Walsh with a clenched fist. "That is some kind of foul."

"Suck it up, will you." Sean gave the gurney another push. "I don't like lingering with that door open."

"Oh. Right." Craig's face had lost some of its color, but he regained his composure enough to take the other end of the gurney and steer it into the room. That done, he scurried around the box and joined Sean near the door.

"Aren't you forgetting something?" Sean glanced nervously around the room, his gaze falling on a second door opposite the first. This one was wide but short, almost like a large cat flap, half the height of the other door. It had no hinges or locks but instead sat in a pair of grooves, one on each side of the frame, to allow it to slip upward like a hatch. It was heavy, made of thick stone, with the bottom resting in a third groove to stop anyone from prying it open manually. The only way to do that was with the thick rope secured to the top, which ran to a pulley, then across the ceiling to a second pulley, before disappearing through the wall next to the door they had entered from.

"I don't think so," Craig said, casting his own fearful glance toward the closed door.

"The lid," Sean said. "Get the other end."

"Ah." Craig hurried back to the other side of the gurney and together they lifted the lid and leaned it against the wall. Tom Walsh, his suit now crumpled, glared up at them with cold, dead eyes.

"Let's get out of here." Sean was already backing up. He waited for Craig to join him and then pulled the outer door closed with a sigh of relief. When the padlock was back on, he felt his stress level go down. He also felt one step closer to that pint.

Still, there was one task left.

The end of the rope hung loose from a final pulley next to the door. Sean spit on his hands, then gripped it high up, leaving enough room for Craig to scoot near and take hold lower down.

Together they pulled.

From the room where Tom Walsh lay, came a grinding, torturous screech as the inner door lifted in its grooves. When they could pull the rope no more, Sean quickly secured it to a cleat attached to the wall, wrapping the cord tight and weaving it into a perfect cleat hitch to make sure the inner door stayed open.

"Thank heaven, we're done." Craig rubbed his hands together. "Now let's get back up top. I don't want to be here when it comes for Tom."

"Agreed." Sean was already turning to hurry back along the tunnel. "You know what, Craig, I've been thinking on what you said about getting away from Clareconnell."

"Coming around to my point of view, are you." Craig couldn't help but grin even though he was panting as he all but ran back to the safety of the church.

"I think I might be." Sean glanced over his shoulder, back toward the locked door. "When my time comes, I'd much rather be food for worms in Dublin, than a feast down here for whatever's about to take our Tom…"

TEN

"YOU THINK Robert and Astrid are down there?" Decker shined his flashlight into the darkness and peered beyond the carved door.

"I don't think it, I know it," Hunt said, pointing to a double set of footprints pressed into the dust and dirt of five hundred years that had settled on the floor of the tunnel beyond the door. "Those are the impressions of modern sneakers, and I'll wager no one else has been down here in living memory. Astrid and Robert came this way."

"And they didn't come back," Rory added. "The footprints only travel in one direction."

"Which means we must go in after them." Hunt was already striding past the door. "I'll warn you all to keep close and pay attention to your surroundings. We have no idea what lies beyond here, but since we've already lost two people, we can assume the way ahead is treacherous."

"I'd feel happier with more light at our disposal," Colum said. "We should go back to the village and get adequate equipment for a search and rescue."

"We're here now." Hunt waved the others to follow him and started down the tunnel. "Let's see what we're dealing with. We can always return to the surface if it's too dangerous, but I hate to think of Robert and Astrid alone down here a minute longer than necessary."

"This tunnel is incredible," Rory said as they walked. "Look at the vaulting on the ceiling. It must be eight hundred years old if it's a day. Just breathtaking."

"I can't believe this has been down here all this time, and no one knew until now." Colum waved his flashlight over the ground ahead of them. The beam picked up more footprints, some occasional debris where parts of the wall had crumbled, and then, up ahead, a second door. This one, made of rough, rotten wood, was the exact opposite of the first. It stood open, although Decker suspected that time had done this rather than the lost archaeologists.

"This just keeps getting more interesting." There was a tinge of excitement in Rory's voice.

"I'll remind you that we are not here to sightsee," Hunt said as they reached the door. "There will be plenty of time for that later."

Decker drew level with Hunt and peered beyond the doorway. Where the tunnel was manmade, constructed with blocks of ancient granite, the space ahead of them was not. When he swung his flashlight beam through the door, Decker saw a cave trailing off into darkness. "A natural cave system. I wonder how far it goes?"

"Let's find out." Hunt took the second flashlight from Colum, then stepped across the threshold. "Watch your step, folks. I don't want any accidents."

The cave was narrow at first, the ceiling only a foot above their heads, but as they continued it widened, even as it sloped further into the underworld. After a while they came to a fork where two tunnels rambled off in different directions. They stopped. Hunt examined each path. Then, without uttering a word, he took off again down the right-hand tunnel. They continued on for a few more minutes, then Decker saw something up ahead, laying in their path. He trained his flashlight on it and was shocked to see a skull staring back at him.

"Human remains," Hunt said, casting the beam of his own flashlight wide and finding other bones. "At least one body, maybe parts of more than one."

"Wow." Rory raced ahead and stopped, hovering over the skull with a look of glee. "I don't believe it."

"Please tell me that skull doesn't belong to Robert or Astrid," Colum said, his eyes wide.

"No. It would take decades, and maybe even longer, to skeletonize a corpse down here." Hunt knelt down next to the skull and studied it. "These remains are centuries old. Look how the skull's surface has deteriorated."

Decker turned away from the skull and wandered toward the other bones. He spied something flat and dark lying next to what looked like a broken tibia. At first, he could not identify it, but then he realized what he was looking at. He played the flashlight beam over it, noting the shrunken, dry leather and familiar shape. "I have a sandal over here."

Rory bounded over. He peered at it, overwhelmed with excitement. "Oh, my goodness. This is stunning. I can't wait to get it back to the surface for a proper examination."

Decker turned his attention to the broken tibia. He'd seen something else, and it disturbed him. "Look at the markings on here," he said, pointing out several parallel rows of gouges on the bone's surface. "This looks like it was gnawed on."

"Rats?" Colum said, glancing around.

"No." Rory was serious now, his face taut. "The marks are too large and deep. Whatever did this was bigger than a rat. A lot bigger."

"What would be bigger than a rat down here?" Colum asked.

"An excellent question. Regardless, given the age of these remains it's long gone." Hunt straightened up and scratched his head. "We should keep moving. We can come back later and make a more thorough examination of the site."

"And for the love of God, be careful," Rory exclaimed as Hunt took off again, picking his way through the mess of scattered bones with the others following behind. "Try not to step on anything."

"Thanks for pointing out the obvious." Colum placed a tentative foot between a rib and several vertebrae that lay half buried. He shuddered. "The last thing I want to do is step on any of this. It's creeping me out, to be honest."

"You were a Ranger in the Irish Defense Force before you signed up with us," Hunt said over his shoulder as they cleared the bone field. "Surely you're not afraid of a few old bones."

"Don't be putting words in my mouth. I never said I was afraid," Colum replied. "I just don't like skeletons, that's all."

"Well, you'd better get used to them," Rory said with a chuckle. "This is an archeological expedition. Bones are kind of our thing."

"Not my thing." Colum pushed past Rory and joined Hunt.

They were deep in the caves now. Decker could feel the air getting colder as they moved further underground. It was like walking into a freezer. He wished he'd brought the sweater Hunt's men had purchased for him. After a few minutes, the cave widened into a long, low cavern. The sound of running water reached his ears. An underground stream, perhaps. He glanced around, but he couldn't tell where it was coming from.

Adam Hunt had figured it out, though. He raced across the cavern, sweeping his flashlight beam across the ground, until there was no more ground to shine it on. Here the cavern fell away into a steep-walled abyss.

Decker peered over and pointed his own light down. Now he saw the stream, barely more than a trickle, meandering along the cave floor thirty feet below. He also saw something else. Laying near the water, arms and legs splayed, was a body.

"Sweet Jesus," Colum breathed. "That's Robert."

ELEVEN

"ROBERT. CAN YOU HEAR ME?" Hunt shouted over the ledge, trying in vain to get a response from the prone man.

"It's no good," Colum said. "I think he might be dead."

"How can we get down there?" Rory asked. "I don't see a path."

Decker studied their surroundings. The chasm was sheer, with plunging walls that provided little in the way of direct access. "The water must go somewhere, which means there may be access further into the caves, but it could take days, or even weeks to find it."

"Assuming a way down exists at all," Hunt said. "The water might continue into places too small for a person to navigate. There's nothing for it. We must make our way back to the surface and find climbing gear if we want to reach Robert."

"What about Astrid?" Colum asked. "She's down here somewhere too. We can't leave before we find her."

"And we can't assume that Robert is dead." Hunt stepped away from the edge. "He may merely be unconscious. We would be derelict in our duty to conclude he's beyond help without making sure."

"You go back to the surface then. Take Rory with you. I'll stay down here with John and we'll keep searching for Astrid until you return."

Hunt shook his head. "No. That's far too dangerous. I will not risk losing more people. We'll return to the surface together and search for ropes."

"And if there aren't any?" Colum asked.

"Then we'll drive back into town and summon help. We must give Robert every chance."

"Look, I know you think he could still be alive," Colum said, his voice hard. "But it's unlikely given the height of his fall and the fact that he isn't responding. Trust me, I've seen situations like this before. He's gone. We need to find Astrid. She's the important one now."

"I appreciate the input, Colum." Hunt rested a hand on the other man's shoulder. "I honestly do. Your military experience is why we recruited you, but there's still a chain of command, and I've made my decision."

"Fair enough." Colum nodded. He turned away from the precipice. "We'd better be going then. Every minute we waste is a minute lost."

They left the chasm behind and hurried back through the cave until the monastery's crypt came into view once more. They reached the outer room and ascended the staircase, going up one by one to put less stress on the old structure. Finally, once they were all above ground again, Hunt led them to the archaeologist's tent, where they searched for ropes. They didn't find any.

"I didn't think we'd have any luck," Rory said as they stood around looking at the meagre tools and artifacts stashed under the canvas. "This was supposed to be a standard surface excavation. Robert and Astrid weren't expecting to find a cave system, so they wouldn't have requisitioned any climbing gear."

"We're off to the village then," Colum said.

"Not all of us." Hunt motioned to Decker. "Just John and me. I want the pair of you to wait here."

"I thought you didn't want us to stay," Colum said.

"No. That isn't what I said." Hunt placed his flashlight on the table. "I don't want you searching the caves alone, but I think someone needs to stay close to the entrance in case Astrid finds her way back to the surface. She may need medical attention."

Colum scowled. "And what do we do if she does? Walk her back to the village?"

Hunt knelt and reached under the table. He came back up with a woman's purse. He opened it and tipped the contents out. A jumble of items cascaded onto the table. Lipstick, mascara, a small black address book, her cell phone, and a set of car keys. He took these and offered them to Colum. "I guess we're lucky that Astrid drove, otherwise these might be in Robert's pocket at the bottom of that chasm."

"I suppose so." Colum took the keys, then dug into his pocket and passed Hunt the Land Rover's key fob. "We'll hang tight then, but don't take too long. I'm anxious to find Astrid."

"We all are, buddy." Hunt turned and slapped Decker on the back. "You ready?"

"Sure," Decker said.

"Great." Hunt threw him the fob. "You're driving."

TWELVE

THEY DROVE into town and went straight to the local Garda station; which Hunt had identified as the best place to get the climbing equipment they needed. Decker agreed with him. But when they arrived at the Garda station – which was nothing more than a converted cottage – they found it locked up and empty.

"This is odd." Hunt rattled the door in frustration. "You'd think someone would be on duty."

"Small town," Decker said. He pointed to a sign affixed to the window with *a number to call in case of emergency after hours.* Decker took out the cell phone Hunt had given him and dialed. It rang twice, then a voice with a thick Irish brogue answered. Decker explained their situation, listened to the response, and then hung up. "He's at the pub."

"What?" Hunt shook his head in disbelief. "It's a bit early for the village cop to be knocking them back, don't you think?"

"There was a funeral today," Decker explained. "We passed it on the way up to the monastery. He's paying his respects."

"He should be here in case someone needs him."

"I think everyone who might need him is in the pub right

alongside of him by the sound of it," Decker replied. "Except for us, that is."

"We'd better be off to the pub then." Hunt was already striding down the street toward the Claddagh Arms. When they got there, Decker's assertion proved to be right. The place was so packed they could barely open the doors.

"Bit different to breakfast this morning, huh?" Decker observed, pushing his way inside. "The entire village must be in here."

"Funerals are good business, I guess." Hunt glanced around. "See anyone that looks like a cop?"

"Nope." Decker made his way to the bar and summoned Harry, the landlord. After a brief discussion, he turned to Hunt. "The local police sergeant is in the snug. He's not in uniform, but we'll know him by his ginger hair, apparently."

"The snug." Hunt was already pushing back through the crowd toward a small room near the stairs. "He's not making this easy, is he?"

"Not in the least." Decker followed along and soon they found the snug which was, just as the name suggested, snug. And sitting there at the closer of two small tables, was the local representative of Garda Síochán—as the police in Ireland were known—his flaming red curly hair unmistakable.

"Can I help you, gentlemen?" he said as they approached. "I assume you're the fellas that called me."

"We are," Hunt said, introducing himself and Decker.

"Sergeant Aiden Byrne, at your service."

"Pleased to make your acquaintance," Hunt said, watching the sergeant sink the dregs of a pint of Guinness. Judging by the empties crowding the table, it was far from his first. "Do you have what we need?"

Sergeant Byrne nodded. "I have a box of climbing gear and some ropes back at the station." He stood and scooted around the table in the direction of the front door. "Not sure how good it is, mind you. Only used it once, and that was ten years ago when young Michael O'Hare got stuck trying to climb into a pit at the quarry. You have a car?"

"Yes." Decker nodded.

"Good. You're driving. I'm not sure I have the capacity at this moment."

Hunt and Decker exchanged glances.

"Is there someone a little less inebriated who could assist us?" Decker asked.

"Like who?" Byrne threw his arms up. "Gordon Wallace, the butcher perhaps? Or maybe the postman? There's one cop in this village, and you're looking at him."

"Just asking," Decker said as they pushed back through the packed bar.

"Well don't. I've responded to calls with more Guinness than this in me, don't you know? Besides, Gordon's been shitfaced since an hour after the pub opened. He'll be no good to you."

"Can we just focus on the ropes?" Hunt asked as they left the pub behind and hurried back toward the Garda station and their car. "We're in a hurry here."

"Give me a minute," Byrne said when they arrived. He unlocked the door and disappeared inside. After a few minutes he returned, carrying a bulky wooden crate. A pair of coiled ropes were slung over one shoulder.

Decker opened the back of the Land Rover and Byrne dumped the items inside. That done, he went around to the front of the car and climbed into the driver's seat. As soon as the others were in, with Hunt next to him in the passenger seat, and Sergeant Byrne in the back, Decker started the engine and swung around in the road, pointing the car back in the monastery's direction.

As they drove, the sergeant leaned forward, inserting his head between the seats. "I don't suppose you boys would mind telling me what organization you're with?"

"Why?" Hunt glanced back at Byrne.

"I like to know who's running around my village, that's all."

Hunt drew a long breath and rubbed the day-old stubble on his chin. "Before I answer that, I must swear you to secrecy. It's very important that our presence here remains low key."

"Well now, that rather depends on whose authority you're asking me to keep that secret."

"How about the Irish government, for a start," Hunt said. "We are operating with their full support."

"Are you now?" Byrne nodded. "In that case, I suppose I can be discreet."

"Very well." Hunt paused for dramatic effect. "We're working under the auspices of the United Nations Educational, Scientific and Cultural Organization. UNESCO for short. We're in the village to evaluate the monastery as a cultural heritage site. If it's approved, it would mean that your village will benefit from increased tourism and a prominent place in world cultural history."

"Really?"

"Indeed." Hunt nodded. "But we must keep it under our hats since nothing is official yet."

Decker shot Hunt a quizzical glance but said nothing.

When they arrived at the monastery, he parked next to the archeologist's still unmoved car, and waited while Sergeant Byrne grabbed the box of climbing gear and set off toward the area where Colum and Rory lingered. Decker picked up the ropes and turned to Hunt. "The Irish government? UNESCO? You think he bought all that cultural heritage bullshit?"

"I think he lapped it up," Hunt said. "But just to be sure, I threw in that line about tourism. The prospect of money has a way of keeping people eager."

Decker started in the tent's direction. "You realize he won't keep a word of what you said confidential, right? The minute he gets back to that pub, the entire village will know."

"I expect as much." Hunt smiled. "If everyone thinks we're only here to declare their monastery a heritage site, they won't ask too many questions."

THIRTEEN

DECKER FOLLOWED Adam Hunt underground for the second time that day. Since the box of climbing gear was too heavy to take down into the crypt, they opened it and took only what they needed, including carabiners, a harness, and two more flashlights. They left the rest at the surface.

Once everyone was underground, they hurried through the first rooms and into the caves, ignoring the sergeant's exclamations of surprise when he saw what lay beneath the ruins. When they came to the spot where the old bones lay scattered across the ground, Byrne stopped, his eyes wide with shock.

"You didn't tell me you found human remains," he said, refusing to move any further.

"I didn't feel it was relevant," Decker said. "These bones are hundreds of years old."

Rory shone a flashlight over the ground. "I'll bet they washed out of the crypt during a water event. These caves probably flood during heavy rains."

"We're wasting time," Hunt said. "We need to reach Robert and assess the situation."

"It's not safe here." Byrne looked back over his shoulder in the direction from which they had come.

"It's safe enough for us to continue, I assure you." Hunt was eager to get moving. "If you want to stay here, that's your prerogative, but we're moving on."

"I'm coming." Byrne picked his way through the bones. "We shouldn't linger down here longer than necessary though."

Decker noticed that the sergeant moved a little faster now, keeping close to Hunt. Every so often he cast a wary glance backwards. Decker couldn't tell if he was making sure the group was together, or if he was expecting to see something there, in the darkness beyond their flashlights. When they reached the cavern, Colum took a coil of rope and hurried to the chasm. He uncoiled a length and searched until he found a large boulder sticking up out of the ground five feet from the edge. He pushed against it, testing to make sure the rock would not budge, and then wrapped one end of the rope around it.

"You need any help?" Decker asked.

"I've got it covered." Colum tied the rope in a girth hitch and ran the loop to the edge of the chasm. Next, he used a carabiner and attached the climbing rope. He pulled on the entire setup, tugging to make sure it was safe, then dropped the rope over the edge. Then he turned to Decker. "You climb?"

"A little, back in the day." Decker suspected that Colum's experience was far greater than his, which comprised a few recreational climbs at a summer camp when he was in his teens.

"Good," Colum said. "I'm going to go down there and check on Robert. If anything happens, or I need backup, you're my man."

"Got it." Decker hoped he wouldn't need to climb down, but if the situation called for it, he would be ready.

Hunt and Rory stepped close to the edge to watch the descent. Sergeant Byrne lingered behind. Colum made one last check of the ropes, and then he stepped over into the abyss.

For three gut wrenching minutes Colum climbed down, the flashlight, now clipped to his belt, bobbing and throwing wild beams of light across the roof and opposite walls. Then he reached the bottom and released the rope. Wasting no time, he sprinted across to the spot where Robert lay sprawled and kneeled beside him, checking for a pulse. After what seemed an eternity he stood and looked up at the faces peering over the rim. Decker didn't need to hear what he was about to say to know it was hopeless. Colum's posture and slumped shoulders said it all.

"He's gone." Colum shouted, the words echoing off the cavern walls. "I'm coming back up."

Hunt cursed and turned away.

Decker stepped away from the edge and checked the hitch to make sure it was still secure. When he returned, Colum was already making his ascent. No one spoke until the ex-army ranger clambered back up out of the chasm and rejoined them, then Hunt addressed the group.

"There's nothing more we can do for Robert, I'm sad to say, but Astrid is still down here somewhere, and it is now imperative that we find her."

"That might be easier said than done," Colum said, glancing around at the three unexplored openings that led away from the cavern. "This place is most likely a labyrinth. Heaven alone knows how far it goes and how many caves are down here."

"She can't have gotten far," Decker said. "Once Robert fell, the logical reaction would be to attempt a return to the surface for help."

"We know that didn't happen," Hunt said. "Her car is still here."

"Where did she go, then?" Decker asked, voicing what they were all thinking.

"The only logical conclusion is that she ventured deeper into the caves, although why she would do that is anyone's guess," Hunt said. "Regardless, it looks like we have no choice but to go deeper ourselves, and search for her."

"I don't think that will be necessary," Decker said, his gaze drifting past the group, to a figure stumbling from the caves. "It looks like she might have found us."

FOURTEEN

"DO you think Astrid will be alright?" Rory asked, nervously biting a fingernail as they waited outside her room at the Claddagh arms for the local doctor—a portly man whom Sergeant Byrne had dragged up from the pub—to complete his examination.

Hunt was typing an email on his phone, pecking at the screen with one fingertip, possibly updating his superiors back in the States with regard to the unfortunate turn of events and Robert McCray's death. Now he tucked the phone back into his pocket and looked up. "She was in those caves for at least twenty-four hours. I am sure she's dehydrated. Further than that, we will have to wait for the good doctor's prognosis."

Decker leaned against the wall and wondered how much longer this would take. It had been more than two hours since Astrid had found them in the cavern. At first, she seemed disoriented, barely able to recognize her surroundings, but when she got above ground her distress faded to a barely perceptible unease. The group split up, Colum driving the rental VW back to town along with Rory, while Hunt and Decker took Astrid and sergeant Byrne in the Land Rover. She sat in the car on the way back, silent and brooding, and offered no explanation regarding what had occurred in the caves, despite Hunt's attempts to question her. In the end he had given up, no doubt assuming she would talk in her own time.

Sergeant Byrne was nowhere in sight. Having determined that there were no physical injuries, and that an actual crime did not appear to have been committed, he excused himself and returned to the barroom under the guise of supporting the family of the deceased man buried that morning. Decker assumed it was more to do with the beer that still flowed copiously below.

When the bedroom door finally opened, and Doctor Winslow emerged, he was met with a barrage of questions from both Colum and Rory.

The doctor held up a hand. "One at a time, please."

"Sorry," Colum said. "We're worried about her, that's all."

"How is she, doc?" Hunt asked, peering past the doctor into the room beyond, where Astrid lay in bed with the covers pulled up to her neck. "Is it bad?"

"No. She's very lucky." The doctor pulled the door closed, cutting off their view of the room. "There are several caves in the area, mostly small systems that don't go too deep. But there are a few, like the one you've discovered under the monastery, that are much bigger. One thing they all have in common, though, is that they are dangerous. Astrid is lucky she didn't fall into a chasm like her colleague, or get lost in the dark never to make it back to the surface."

"But physically, is she injured?" Colum asked.

"Some cuts and bruises," the doctor said. "She has a rather nasty bump on her head and a mild concussion. She's also a little dehydrated. She should rest for at least twenty-four hours, and we'll take it from there."

"Can we talk to her?" Hunt asked, looking anxiously at the closed door. "I must find out what happened down there."

"That will have to wait, I'm afraid," The doctor said. "She's in no state for an interrogation."

"I think interrogation is a bit of a strong word."

"My apologies." The doctor smiled. "I meant no offense. I merely think it would be better if you wait until Miss Hansen has regained her strength. She's been through an ordeal."

"Which is precisely why I wish to talk to her," Hunt replied. Then, when he saw that the doctor was unmoved by his protestations, he relaxed his posture. "Sorry. It's been a trying day, and I'm concerned."

"Understandable." Doctor Winslow stepped past Hunt. "None-the-less, I shall expect you to give her the time she needs to recuperate."

"Naturally." Hunt watched the doctor leave, then turned to the others. "It would seem we will have to wait awhile to get our answers regarding the goings on in that cave."

Colum folded his arms. "Speaking of the cave, when are we going to retrieve Robert's body? It's not right, him being left down there like that in the dark."

"For now, that is where he will have to stay," Hunt said. "We don't have the equipment nor expertise to retrieve him. We also don't have the jurisdiction."

"One phone call stateside would take care of any jurisdiction issue."

"Not going to happen, Colum. We're under the radar here, and I intend to keep it that way," Hunt replied. "Besides, Cave Rescue will be here in the morning. Sergeant Byrne called them from the car on the way back to the village. By tomorrow lunchtime we'll have Robert."

"And we might also have some answers," Decker said, glancing toward Astrid's closed door. "I for one, am very curious how a simple Archeological expedition ended up with one person lost for twenty-four hours underground, and their partner dead."

FIFTEEN

IT WAS late in the evening. Decker occupied a table in the Claddagh's barroom and sipped a cold pint. The pub was still busy, but nothing like the hectic crush earlier in the day when the entire village, it seemed, had turned out to pay their respects. Regardless, a smattering of soused villagers refused to call it a night. Sergeant Byrne was not among them, Decker noted with relief.

Hunt had been prudent in fabricating a story to cover for their presence in the village. As Decker expected, Byrne proved unable to keep their activities at the monastery a secret, and Decker found himself returning curious, and sometimes guarded, stares. It didn't take long for one of the locals, no doubt buoyed by Dutch courage, to approach him.

"Mind if I sit down?" The man held two pints of dark beer in his hand. He held one out toward Decker. "I brought you a fresh pint since yours is looking a smidge empty."

Decker glanced down at his glass, which was a little under half-full. He motioned toward a chair. "Be my guest."

"Thank you." The man eased into a seat and placed the pints on the table. From across the room, still propping up the bar, the man's friend looked on. "I'm Sean." He nodded toward the bar. "My mate over there is Craig. He's a tad shy, so you'll have to excuse him."

"John Decker."

Sean nodded. "We don't get many visitors around here. You just passing through?"

"We'll be in town a few days." Decker shifted in his chair. He had a feeling Sean knew exactly why they were in the village. "I'm sure you've heard of the archeological expedition up at the monastery."

"I have." Sean cast a furtive glance around the bar and then leaned close. He spoke in a low voice. "I've got to tell you, there's a lot of curiosity about what exactly is going on up there."

"There's really isn't much to tell," Decker said. "It's a simple dig, nothing more."

"Is that so?" Sean took a long swig of his beer and narrowed his eyes. "Word is you found a body. Seems like one of the archaeologists went and fell into a ravine in some caves you found under the ruin. Got himself killed."

"I'm not at liberty to comment on that." Decker lifted his own glass. It appeared that Sergeant Byrne had been mighty liberal in his conversations upon their return to the village, relaying even those details which should have remained confidential.

"It's true then." Sean's lips were a thin line.

"Yes." Decker could see no point in holding back information which appeared to be common knowledge already. "It's true. It was an accident, nothing more."

"I assumed as much." Sean had finished his pint. "You'll be calling in the cave rescue, I suppose."

"First thing in the morning."

"Best not to leave him down there under the circumstances." Sean stood and picked up his empty glass. He took a step towards the bar, then turned back to Decker. "A word of advice. Don't linger too long in those caves. I wouldn't want there to be any more accidents."

Decker watched Sean approach the bar and rejoin his friend. There was an ominous subtext to the Irishman's words, a warning that went beyond the obvious dangers of the caves. He sensed that Sean was keeping his own secrets, but what they were Decker could not guess.

SIXTEEN

SEAN LEFT the Claddagh Arms thirty minutes after Harry called time. He was buzzed. He'd consumed more than he should've, and now the beer was flowing through his veins, gently numbing his senses. The village was quiet. As he walked up Winslow Road, he barely saw a soul.

He passed the butcher's shop, and the small supermarket where he had worked as a teen many years ago, stocking shelves and bagging groceries. Up ahead was the church. The memory of what he and Craig had done earlier pushed its way back into Sean's mind despite his inebriation. He wondered if the sight of Tom Walsh's dead face, those milky glazed eyes staring up at him out of the coffin, would ever leave him. He would have nightmares tonight, he was sure.

It was starting to rain. A steady drizzle that soaked him to the bone. He pulled his coat close and lowered his head. It was as if even the weather was mourning the passing of Tom Walsh.

Sean was at the end of the village now. It was another mile's walk to his cottage on the edge of a vast expanse of untended fields. At one time his family had farmed this land, but not anymore. Cheap prices from overseas and the emergence of corporate farming had pinched profits until there was barely a penny to be had. If his father could've seen just how bad things had gotten, he would've shed a tear or two, but Sean's dad had gone the way of Tom Walsh many years ago. That thought disturbed him more than the decline of the farm, and so he did his best to push it from his mind and concentrate on the task at hand.

The road was dark beyond the village and there was no sidewalk. Sean hugged the grass verge as he walked. It was unlikely he would encounter a car, but it wasn't unknown for a vehicle to come barreling down the lanes even at this time of night and there was no guarantee the driver would see him. Sean did not want to spend the night injured in a ditch. If he hadn't intended to drink all day at the Claddagh, he would have taken his own car to the funeral for sure. Not that the walk back to the cottage bothered him. He'd done it many times after a session in the pub. Still, tonight felt different. He was on edge. When there hadn't been a death in the village for a while, it was easy to forget about what lay beneath the church, but on evenings such as this his imagination ran wild. Which was why he hurried his step, eager to be safely behind his own front door.

The village was far behind Sean now. The weak glow from its streetlamps nothing more than a dull yellow shimmer in the distance. There was still half a mile to walk, and Sean's unease was growing. It wasn't just that the alcohol was wearing off, or that the drizzling rain had stopped, and the cool summer breeze ebbed away to nothing. It was too quiet even for the Irish countryside. Something was not right.

Sean stopped.

He glanced around, nervous.

Across the rolling fields, next to a stand of trees, he could see the dim outline of a building, barely perceptible against the darkness. This would be his neighbor, Ed McGrath. Their cottages were separated by several acres of farmland and a brook that swelled into a veritable river during winter. No light shone from within the building's windows. Ed McGrath was probably asleep already.

Sean took a faltering step forward. His sense of unease was growing. Aiden Byrne had been in the pub earlier, talking about the caves under the monastery. He'd also mentioned the human remains that littered the floor. The consensus among the visitors from UNESCO was that the bones were washed into the caves by floodwaters, but Sean knew better. The bones might be ancient, but it was not a flood that put them there, he was sure. That made him wonder if the caves under the monastery ran all the way to the village, and the room in which they had left Tom Walsh.

Sean's heart was beating fast now. He felt exposed on the lonely road. Then, as if to validate his unease, a rustle came from the hedgerow that lined the road to his right. It was a slight sound, nothing more than a scrabbling in the undergrowth. Then as quickly as it had come, it was gone again.

Sean held his breath and listened, ears straining to pick up the sound again, but he heard nothing now. It was, he told himself, probably just a rabbit scurrying to its burrow, or a fox skulking the area for prey. He released his pent-up breath and started down the road again, Increasing his speed from a walk to a jog.

Then the sound came again.

This time it was louder and closer.

Sean's throat tightened with fear. This was bigger than a rabbit or even a fox. He peered to his right, eyes searching the undergrowth, but he saw nothing. It was there though, he knew, following along beside him.

Sean resisted the urge to run. "Who's there?" He said in a trembling voice.

The words hung in the air, unanswered.

"I have a knife on me." This was a lie. Sean did not have a knife, but speaking the words made him feel safer. At least until he heard the rustling again.

Any bravado Sean gained with his words quickly left him. He abandoned the jog and broke into a run, his feet smacking the pavement as he sprinted toward his cottage and safety.

Whatever was stalking him in the bushes kept pace, following along no matter how fast he ran. Sean's breath came in short, sharp gasps. He was tearing along in a blind panic now, desperate to escape. Thoughts of what lay below the church back in Clareconnell only heightened his dread.

He could see his cottage up ahead now. If he had not been so winded, he would have cried with relief.

His pursuer was crashing through the bushes, abandoning all attempts at stealth. Sean tensed, expecting to be leapt upon from the undergrowth at any moment. He was not. Instead, he reached his front door, scrabbling to find his keys. He almost dropped them trying to open the door, but then he was inside and slamming it shut behind him. He leaned against the wall and gulped in deep gasps of air. He stayed that way for a few moments while his panic subsided. When he went to the window, pulled the curtain back and looked out, the countryside was empty and peaceful. Whatever had chased him was nowhere to be seen.

SEVENTEEN

DECKER STOOD at the window in his room at the Claddagh Arms pub and watched the first rays of golden sunlight spill across the Irish countryside. He'd risen early, unable to sleep thanks to his body clock, which stubbornly refused to adapt to this new time zone five hours ahead of Eastern seaboard time. Once dressed he hurried downstairs to find that Hunt, Rory, and Colum, had once again beat him to breakfast. He joined them and ordered the same meal as the previous day, ignoring Colum's bemused smirk. This time when the food came, he readily handed the Irishman the white and black puddings.

"Have you looked in on Astrid this morning?" Decker asked.

"There isn't much change from last night, unfortunately," Hunt said. "She was still sleeping when I poked my head inside the room, and I didn't want to wake her."

Colum, shoveling food into his mouth, talked between bites. "I sure would like to know what went on in those caves."

"We all would." Hunt motioned to Harry for a refill of his empty coffee cup, and then addressed Decker. "I have some news regarding your recent skirmish in the Florida Woodlands."

"Really?" Decker raised an eyebrow. Hunt had shown little interest in his Florida adventure up to this point. In fact, this was the first time he'd mentioned it since showing up at Decker's hotel room door in Tampa several days before.

"Indeed." Hunt leaned back in his chair. "I sent a team to evaluate the situation. It seemed like the prudent thing to do under the circumstances."

"And?"

"We recovered what remained of the beast you dispatched with the crane. The subsequent analysis proved most interesting. Your monster was not prehistoric, but was, rather, the result of some very nifty genetic engineering. We even traced the source of that biological tinkering."

"You know where the beast came from?" Decker leaned forward in his chair. "Tell me."

"Someone stole your two-legged crocodilian from a research facility near the Florida border a few years ago. The company chose not to report it to the authorities for fear of losing their funding. How the beast made its way to the Central Florida Woodlands is still not clear, but given the proximity of a rival genetics facility a few miles from Leland, we are working under the assumption that the creature got loose as the result of a botched attempt at industrial espionage. Especially since that facility reported its head geneticist missing around the same time as the theft."

"That makes a lot more sense than a prehistoric creature surviving undetected all the way to modern times," Decker said.

"It also means that Leland is safe, since there appears to have been only one creature, and it was probably unable to breed."

"I'm relieved to hear that." Decker wondered if anyone had told Bill Gibson this news. He'd only been an employee of CUSP for a few days, but he was already aware of their penchant for secrecy.

Rory glanced between the two men with an excited expression on his face. "There was a prehistoric crocodile running around in Florida. That's so cool."

"Only when it isn't trying to eat you," Decker said dryly.

Hunt's phone rang.

He answered, listened for a few moments, then hung up. "Cave Rescue are on their way. They're going to meet us at the ruins in an hour."

"Thank heavens for that." Colum had finished his meal now and was dabbing his mouth with a napkin. "I'll feel better once Robert is out of that cave."

"What's going to happen to the excavation?" Rory asked, concerned.

"That depends on what Astrid says when we talk to her," Hunt replied. "Which I'm hoping will be today. I don't care what that doctor says, we need answers and we need them now."

"Do you think they really found the remains of Grendel?" Rory asked.

"What about the bones we came across in the tunnel yesterday?" Decker said. "Could those be Grendel?"

"I doubt it." Rory shook his head. "Those bones were human and lacking any malformation. Grendel is barely described in the original poem, but the subtext makes clear that Grendel is a monster. A devourer of humankind, to quote the source."

Colum looked up. "Those bones certainly looked like something devoured them. We all saw the teeth marks on that tibia." He chuckled. "Maybe the poor chap was a meal for Grendel."

"Unlikely." Colum's humor appeared lost on Rory. "Grendel was dead by the time the Danes came to Ireland and buried him in that cave," Rory pointed out. "Whatever chewed on that unfortunate individual all those centuries ago was not Beowulf's beast."

"That leads us back to the original question," Colum said. "Did they really find Grendel's resting place?"

"Only Astrid can answer that." Hunt finished his coffee, pushed his chair back, and stood up. He glanced at his watch. "Now gentlemen, we must be on the move if we are to meet Cave Rescue at the ruins. The sooner we get Robert out of that cavern and put this nasty business behind us, the quicker we can get back to the job at hand. Retrieving the bones of Grendel."

EIGHTEEN

SEAN WOKE up with a pounding head. He groaned, rolled out of bed, and staggered to the bathroom where he found a bottle of painkillers in the medicine cabinet. He wrenched the top off, took two, and washed them down with gulps of water from the tap. It was a little after 9 AM, later than he usually rose, and he had work to do, having taken the previous day off to attend the funeral and subsequent piss up in the pub.

He returned to the bedroom and climbed back into bed. He would, he told himself, lay here for just ten more minutes to let his headache subside. He closed his eyes and thought back to the previous day's events. His memories of the morning were clear, hauling Tom Walsh from the church into that dank crypt, and their hasty retreat. After that it got a little murky. An entire afternoon and evening sinking pints in the Claddagh had probably not been the best idea. Every time he went on a session, regardless of the excuse, he swore he would never drink again. That resolution usually lasted about as long as the pub was closed. He struggled to recall the events of the previous night. He remembered talking to Craig at the bar and approaching one of the guests staying in the rooms above, and bending his ear for a while. The man was American. His name was Declan or Dexter, or something like that. After that, things got murky. The next thing he remembered was saying goodnight and staggering out of the pub and up Winslow Road. Then he remembered something else. The uneasy feeling that had come upon him, and the strange rustling sounds emanating from the bushes on the side of the road. He also remembered getting spooked and running full pelt for the safety of his home. Now that he thought about it, he hadn't actually seen anything that would warrant such a reaction. And yet whatever was in the bushes had followed him, keeping pace. That didn't mean it was anything dangerous, though. Now, in the cold light of day, he felt a little foolish. It probably had just been a prowling fox. Still, his sense of unease remained.

Sean's headache was abating now, at least a little. He climbed back out of bed, got dressed, and went to the kitchen where he made himself a cup of tea. He sat at the table and stared down into the brown liquid, knowing that he should collect his tools and head over to Clamagh Farm, where he'd picked up a few days of carpentry work rebuilding a staircase in the old farmhouse. He was not feeling it today, though. Ever since he'd turned his back on farming his own land, Sean had felt a growing sense of animosity toward those few farmers in the area who were still making a living out of the land. Barry Clamagh had struck a deal with a large poultry processor and converted most of his barns into tight-packed factory chicken coops. The pay was not spectacular, but it kept the lights on. The same company had approached Sean, but he had turned them down. He had no desire to turn his farm into a death camp for genetically altered, obese chickens that could barely stand up under their own steam. It might not have been the best business decision, but if his farm was going to fail, at least it would fail with dignity.

Sean finished his cup of tea and stood up. He put the cup in the sink and was about to grab his car keys, deciding that even though he didn't feel like working, losing a day's pay was not the smartest thing to do, when his phone rang.

It was Ellen Hennessey, Craig's wife.

When he answered, she sounded annoyed.

"Is that no good eejit with you?"

"Craig?"

"Well now, who else would I be talking about?" Ellen made an exasperated tsk sound from the other end of the phone.

"Why would he be with me?" Sean asked.

"Because every time the pair of you get rat-arsed, he crashes at your place and doesn't show his face around here until the next afternoon," Ellen said. "God alone knows what the pair of you get up to all night."

"He's not here." Sean forced his mind back to the previous night. When he'd left the Claddagh, Craig was still there, propping up the bar and pontificating to Harry in a loud voice. "He was still in the pub when I went home."

"Fekin typical." Ellen's voice was rising in pitch. "I bet Harry had a lock-in."

"More than likely." Sean had been to a few of Harry's lock-in's himself. It was not uncommon for the landlord to close up, lock the doors, and then reopen the bar after hours on the down-low for those trusted locals who did not want to call it a night. Sometimes the after-hours boozing could go on until dawn, which was why Sean tried to avoid such situations these days. He drank enough without spending the entire night in the pub. "I'm sure he'll come home when he's ready."

"That's assuming I don't change the locks first," Ellen said. "Do me a favor Sean, if you see Craig, tell him he'd better get his ass home while he still has a wife to come home to."

"I'll do that, Ellen." Sean's headache was getting worse again. He glanced toward the bathroom and the painkillers within. "You take care now."

The phone went dead. Ellen had hung up without bothering to say goodbye. Sean put the phone back in his pocket and stood there, thinking. That Craig had spent the night drinking behind locked doors at the Claddagh made sense. Yet there had been no talk of a lock-in, and Harry always invited him to such events. The nagging unease that had been plaguing him since his terrified sprint home the previous evening had returned. Something was not right. Sean had a bad feeling there was trouble ahead.

NINETEEN

CAVE RESCUE WAS ALREADY WAITING when Decker and the others arrived at the monastery ruins. Two large-set men wearing orange coveralls and hard hats stood next to a white Land Rover with the words Cave Rescue written on the side in red lettering. Sergeant Byrne lingered nearby. They pulled up in the Land Rover and parked next to the Clareconnell police car. When they got out the sergeant wasted no time introducing them to the rescuers, who turned out to be a pair of brothers, Sam and Artie Wallace, from the neighboring town. The sergeant explained that the rescue service was purely voluntary, so the quicker they took care of things, the better. He didn't want to take up more of their time than was necessary.

"Shall we get going then," Artie said, after they finished the introductions. He opened the back of the Land Rover and took out climbing gear that appeared to be in much better condition than the equipment the sergeant had provided to Hunt the previous day. He slung several coils of nylon rope over his shoulder, picked up a sling, and hitched a bag over his other shoulder. His brother pulled out an orange collapsible emergency stretcher and together the pair made their way toward the interior of the ruin.

"After you." The sergeant motioned for Decker, Hunt, and the others to follow along, and then he fell in at the rear.

"Where exactly is the body," Sam asked, peering down into the dark hole. He reached up and activated a light attached to his hard hat. The beam pierced the blackness, illuminating the spiral stone steps that wound down into the crypt. "I have to say, this is the first time that I've been called to a cave that came with its own stairs. If everything is this easy, we'll be done in a jiffy."

"I wouldn't get too excited, boys," the sergeant said. "Once you get past the crypt, there's a substantial cave system."

"The body is in a cavern, at the bottom of a deep chasm," Decker said.

"I thought it was too good to be true." Sam moved toward the crypt entrance. "I'll go down first and the rest of you follow behind. Artie will lead up the rear."

"I think if it's all the same with you guys, I'll stay up top," the sergeant said, giving the hole in the ground a nervous glance.

"Don't you think you should be there, Sergeant?" Artie looked surprised. "You are the only representative of local law enforcement. How are you going to write up the report if you are not there when we retrieve the body?"

"It's an open and shut case," the sergeant said, with a weak smile. "A tragic accident, nothing more. I've already examined the scene and I don't need any more information to complete my paperwork. Besides, it makes sense to stay topside so that if anything else goes wrong, I can summon help."

"If the man doesn't want to go, then I guess he can stay here." Hunt shook his head. "The last thing we need down there is an inexperienced amateur plodding around, anyway."

The sergeant glared at Hunt but said nothing.

"Right-ho." Sam shrugged. He stepped down onto the first step. "Just to be on the safe side, we'll go down one by one. The steps look mighty old, and I'd hate for them to collapse on us. Once I'm down, I'll call up for the next person."

Decker watched as Sam disappeared into the hole. A few

moments later, his voice drifted back up. He'd made it to the bottom. Hunt went next. Rory and Colum followed on, until Decker, Artie, and the sergeant were the only ones left above ground. Decker took one last glance around, noting how relieved the sergeant looked, knowing that he wouldn't have to follow them in, and then started down the stairs and into the darkness below.

TWENTY

FATHER PATRICK CLEARY paced back and forth in his church's sacristy. He had been uneasy ever since Sergeant Byrne returned to the pub the previous day talking about the labyrinth discovered underneath the monastery ruins and the archaeologist who had fallen to his death within. There had long been rumors in the village that a cave entrance lay beneath the monastery. It was well known that the monks were the original keepers of the secret the village now guarded. Where that entrance lay had been lost to time and the dimming of the villager's collective memories. Until now, that was. The rediscovery of the monastery's crypt had set tongues wagging. There was a palpable sense of fear among the residents of Clareconnell regarding what lived beneath their feet, and the very real chance that the contingent of visiting archaeologists would discover it. Byrne's over-confident reassurances that all would be fine did little to ease the villager's worries.

The priest was more concerned than most. His church rested above the only other known entrance to the caves and there was little doubt in his mind that the crypt under the monastery connected to the very same tunnels his own subterranean entrance did. He was anxious to check on Tom Walsh and make sure the village's offering had been accepted. This would, he hoped, keep the occupant of the caves distracted long enough to allow the retrieval of the dead archaeologist's body without incident. It had been twenty-four hours since the funeral and Craig should have been at the church fifteen minutes ago to retrieve the empty gurney from the chamber where they had left the body. It was not like Craig to be late.

Father Cleary went over to the landline that sat on a shelf near the sacristy door. He picked up the receiver and dialed the Hennessey residence. That he knew this number off the top of his head was not surprising. The village was small and only a handful of villagers regularly volunteered to perform jobs at the church. Pallbearer duties were among the most needed and least favorite of them all. Few people wanted the task of delivering Clareconnell's newly departed underground. Not only was it a nerve-racking endeavor, but it also served as a reminder of the eventual fate of anyone who remained in the village long enough to die there. Just once, the priest would love to perform a funeral where they took the deceased and buried them in consecrated ground. As long as he remained in Clareconnell, that would not happen, he knew.

The phone rang three times, then went to voicemail.

The priest replaced the receiver. But then a thought struck him. He picked it up again and dialed a different number.

The call was answered this time.

"Father Cleary?" Sean sounded surprised that the priest was calling him. "Did you forget that it's Craig's turn to retrieve the gurney? I did it last September after John O'Garrity's funeral, remember?"

"Sean, my boy, I did not forget. Not at all. Craig was supposed to be here a quarter of an hour ago and there's no sign of him yet. I wondered if you'd seen him. I'm sure the pair of you were in the pub together last night boozing it up."

"You're the second person to call me about Craig today." Sean's voice was laced with concern. "Ellen phoned earlier this morning wanting to know if Craig came back to my place after the Claddagh kicked out. I told her he hadn't. I haven't seen him since last call."

"I see," Father Cleary said. "I don't suppose you'd be available today, would you? I know it's not your turn, but I would appreciate it, as would the Lord."

"Sorry, Father. I'm on a job right now at Barry Clamagh's farm. I'll be out here until evening at least, maybe later. I really want to get this finished so that I can get paid. The electric bill is due and I'm feeling a little tight this month. I can come by after I leave here, though."

"Don't worry yourself." Father Cleary did not want to wait that long.

"Well, the offer is there. Just call if you need me," Sean said. "If Craig doesn't show up soon, try the Claddagh. My guess is that Harry had a lock-in last night and Craig's sleeping it off in one of the rooms above the bar."

"I'll do that, my boy." The priest waited for Sean to say goodbye and then replaced the receiver. If Craig had spent all night inside the Claddagh knocking them back, he would be next to useless even if Cleary could locate him. Sometimes he wished that Harry was a little less congenial. While after hours drinking was technically illegal, Sergeant Byrne did little to discourage the practice. He'd even been known to partake of an all-night session or two himself, right alongside those he was supposed to be admonishing for flouting the law.

There was nothing for it. Father Cleary would have to venture under the church without Craig. The thought of that made his gut clench, but the alternative was waiting for Sean to finish his work at Clamagh Farm. That would take hours, and the priest did not want to leave the door into the caves open for that long. It was not safe. Better to go down there himself and drop the door back into place right now.

Father Cleary made his way from the sacristy, across the altar, and to the small room next to the Lady Chapel. He stepped inside and closed it behind him then hurried down the steps to the chamber beneath the church. He crossed to the tunnel and entered, hurrying along as fast as his legs would carry him. The less time he spent down here, the better. If Craig had bothered to show up, he would not be down here at all.

When he reached the end of the tunnel, Father Cleary came to a halt. He stood looking at the door that blocked his path, a knot of fear writhing in his stomach. He almost turned and fled back to the church, but he knew that would achieve nothing. The priest moved closer, stepping up to the door. He whispered a prayer under his breath and asked God for protection. Then he leaned in close to a peephole installed in the door and peered through.

What he saw drew a gasp of disbelief from the startled priest. He turned and took hold of the tied rope, uncoiling it from the cleat and letting the inner door grind slowly back down into place. When it was fully closed, he unlocked the outer door and opened it. With a fresh prayer upon his lips, Father Cleary stepped across the threshold, ignoring the rotten stench that hung in the air, and stared at the untouched corpse of Tom Walsh.

TWENTY-ONE

SERGEANT BYRNE WATCHED the group disappear down into the opening in the ground. He was relieved that no one had challenged his reluctance to accompany them into the caves. Not that he was afraid. At least that's what he told himself. It was more to do with simple self-preservation. There was no need for so many people to be down there, especially since he knew what lurked in the darkness. That he hadn't bothered to warn them did not worry him. The Cave Rescue people could take care of themselves, and the outsiders were just that. Outsiders. They had no business poking around the ruins in the first place. In fact, if it were up to him, they would never have been granted permission to dig. Except Dublin had issued the permit, and no one bothered to ask his opinion. Besides, he didn't trust Hunt and his clutch of operatives. They claimed to be archaeologists, but with a few exceptions, none of them looked like they made a living scrabbling in the ground. The well-built Irishman, Colum, was ex-military. The way he carried himself, and the way he'd scrambled down the rope to reach the dead archaeologist the previous day, left little doubt in the sergeant's mind. Not to mention the three Americans who'd shown up a couple of nights ago. Only one of them looked like he might fit the bill. Byrne would be surprised if the other two had ever held a trowel, let alone excavated anything. All in all, he didn't trust them as far as he could throw them. He was also not entirely sure the story Hunt had told him in the car on the way to the monastery the previous afternoon was true. For all he knew they could be CIA operatives, although why American spies would be poking around an old ruined monastery was anyone's guess. Either way, he was glad to be up here instead of below ground in the caves with them.

Now that he was alone though, he wasn't sure that he wanted to be up here either. He felt vulnerable. He cast a nervous glance around, searching the barren landscape for anything out of the ordinary. Nothing appeared to be out of place or unusual, yet the nagging sense of unease remained. The wind was picking up now too. Dark storm clouds were scudding across the sky, pushed along by upper-level currents, and the temperature was dropping fast. When they had arrived here, the sun was shining, and the slight breeze provided a welcome respite from the summer heat. Now, as was so often the case in Ireland, the weather was turning. It was almost as if the elements had picked up on the sergeant's mood.

Byrne shivered and took a step backwards.

A little way distant, outside of the main monastery complex, was his car. That seemed like a fine place to whittle away the time until the rest of the group returned from below. Byrne pulled his coat closed and started toward the parked vehicles. When he got there, he wasted no time unlocking his car and climbing in, pulling the door closed.

The unsettled feeling abated a little. Despite this, Byrne glanced into the back seat, just to make sure it was empty.

It was.

He reached out and turned on the radio, the soft rock station that he listened to filling the vehicle with the dulcet tones of Simon and Garfunkel. The music acted like a psychological enema, sweeping away the nagging disquiet. In fact, now that he

82

was safe in the car, he felt a little foolish. Other than the dead man lying in the chasm beneath, which was most likely an accident, there was no sign that anything was amiss. Sure, there were old bones down in the caves, but what did that prove? And even if the remains were connected to the village's dark secret, whatever had befallen that poor individual happened a very long time ago. The caves under the monastery were, Byrne speculated, probably safe.

It was then that his cell phone rang.

Sergeant Byrne jumped. He sat there a moment while his thudding heart quieted, then pulled the phone from his pocket. He looked down at the screen. It was Father Cleary. He reached out and snapped the radio off before answering.

"What is it, Father?" Byrne said, a little too tersely. "I'm kind of busy here."

"Don't take that tone with me, Sergeant." The priest sounded agitated. "I'm the one that baptized you, don't you forget."

"Sorry, Father." Byrne's tone softened. "How can I help you?"

"I just went under the church. Craig was supposed to do it, but he's nowhere to be found. The sot is probably sleeping off a hangover somewhere."

"And?"

"Tom Walsh. It didn't take him." The priest sounded more than agitated now. He sounded afraid.

"What do you mean, it didn't take him? It always takes them."

"Well, it didn't this time." The priest sounded out of breath as if he'd been running. The sergeant speculated that he'd probably run all the way back from the offering chamber. At the priest's ripe old age, that was no mean feat. "This has never happened before."

"You don't need to state the obvious." The sergeant shifted in his seat, his creeping unrest returning.

"What are you going to do about it?"

"I don't think there's anything I *can* do about it."

"Well, we can't just leave poor old Tom down there." The priest's voice cracked as he talked.

"I think that's exactly what we need to do," Byrne said. "Keep the door to the caves open and leave it another night. Maybe it'll come for him then."

"And if it doesn't?"

"We'll deal with that if it happens." The sergeant glanced toward the ruined monastery walls, and the hole in the ground that led to the gloomy crypt. It was taking too long to recover the archaeologist's body. He wished they would hurry so he could get out of this miserable place. To the priest he said: "Check on Tom again in the morning. If he's still there then, call me."

"I don't like this." The priest sounded as spooked as Byrne was. "But I don't suppose we have much choice."

"No, we don't." The sergeant hung up without waiting for the priest to reply. He pushed the phone back into his pocket and peered out through the windshield. There was still no sign of the men that had gone below. He reached out to switch the radio back on but changed his mind. Instead, he turned and locked the car doors. Then he sat in silence and looked out over the rugged, desolate fields, and wondered if there was something out there, unseen, looking back at him.

TWENTY-TWO

IT WAS JUST as cold underground as Decker remembered from their previous trip, but this time he'd possessed the good sense to bring a sweater and now slipped it on. He kept pace with the rest of the group as they navigated their way through the crypt, past the door carved with demons, and into the caves beyond. It was easier to see in the caves now, between the flash-lights the group held, and the lamps attached to the rescue personnel's hard hats. The cave walls were slick and wet with moisture that had seeped from the earth above. There were also more bones down here than Decker had previously realized. The remains found on their first trip into the caves were just one set of bones among many, most of which were buried in the cave floor.

Rory had also noticed the trove of disarticulated remains. At one point he stopped and knelt, brushing away a layer of loose earth from what appeared to be a thigh bone. He lifted it gently and turned it over in his hands, eyes glinting with excitement.

"Incredible," Rory said. "There's enough in these caves to keep an entire team of archaeologists busy for a year."

"This looks more like a killing field than the result of flood-water," Hunt said. "If water had washed the bones into the

85

caves, we would see them everywhere, but they're localized in this one area near the door. There were no bones in the cavern where we found Robert."

"I agree," Rory said. He ran a finger along the length of the thigh bone, stopping at a set of notched grooves on its surface. "These appear to be the result of gnawing, much like the tibia we discovered. Whoever these people were, something appears to have been chewing on them."

"My guess is that they were monks," Decker said. He was peering at an object lying near the cave wall. He bent and retrieved it, holding it up for the others to see. A tarnished and pitted silver crucifix attached to a chain.

"Oh my. Let me see that." Rory all but snatched the crucifix from Decker's hand. "This is beyond wonderful. Who knows what else we'll find when we mount a full excavation down here."

"That's for another day." Hunt was growing impatient. "Our priority is recovering Robert."

"You're right, of course." Rory slipped the crucifix into his pocket. He kneeled and placed the thigh bone back on the ground, careful to position it exactly where he had found it. He stood and brushed his hands off. "I got carried away. This is all so exciting. I can't wait to retrieve samples from these bones and run a carbon-14 dating on them."

"All in good time." Hunt was on the move again, taking the lead now, with the rescue personnel on his heel. "I want to talk to Astrid before we decide on further excavating this site."

"I'm rather keen to hear what Astrid has to say, myself." Rory hurried to keep up, careful not to step on any of the bones as he went.

"Do you think the monastery was using these caves as a burial ground?" Decker asked.

"It doesn't seem likely." Rory shook his head. "There is precedent for cave systems being used in burials. The catacombs under Paris are one example. City leaders turned old quarry tunnels into a mammoth ossuary to hold the bones of at least six-million Parisians. Those bones were neatly stacked and treated with reverence. The remains in this cave are scattered, and it's unlikely that the monks would have wished to bury their dead in such a place. I can't imagine that the caves are consecrated ground. The crypt would be a more likely location for any burials."

"Then how did they get here?" Decker asked. "And what was chewing on them?"

"I don't have an answer to either question," Rory said, as they approached the cavern where Robert's body lay. "But I hope to find out."

The sound of running water was growing louder now. Above them, on the ceiling, stalactites hung down, water dripping off them and pitter-pattering onto the cave floor. When they entered the cavern, Decker looked up and saw even larger stalactite formations thrusting toward the ground from the dark stone above. Here and there, stalagmites inched upward, calcified fingers straining toward their hanging counterparts.

"He's over here." Hunt was striding across the cavern floor in the chasm's direction.

The rescue personnel stopped a few feet from the edge and unloaded their gear, placing the ropes, harness, and stretcher on the ground. "We'll use that boulder as an anchor," Sam said, nodding toward the same rock that Colum had used previously. "It looks stable enough."

Hunt moved toward the chasm's edge. He peered over, then turned back to the group. "I don't think we will need the climbing apparatus."

"Why not?" Colum asked.

"Because he's gone," Decker said, looking down into the chasm where the corpse should have been. Instead, all he saw was a disturbed patch of gravel, and drag marks leading off into the darkness beyond, where a cave entrance yawned. "Someone, or something, has taken Robert."

TWENTY-THREE

SEAN O'MARA WAS HAMMERING in a new stair tread when he became aware that someone was watching him. He turned to find Barry Clamagh at the foot of the stairs, arms folded, and a scowl on his face.

"When are you going to finish this up?" Barry asked. "You've been banging around here all day and you don't look like you're any further on than you were when you started this morning."

"I'll be done by this evening." Sean didn't like people looking over his shoulder while he worked. It made him uncomfortable. Especially when that person was Barry Clamagh. He stood and descended the stairs, pushing past the other man, who seemed disinclined to move out of Sean's way. From somewhere else in the house, Sean could hear Barry's wife talking on the phone. Lucy Clamagh was kinder than her husband, and Sean wondered what she saw in the brutish oaf. He was not a pleasant man to be around, and even less pleasant to work for.

"It's no wonder your farm went bust, if this is your work ethic." Barry watched Sean pick up a fresh box of nails from the pile of supplies near the front door.

"Yeah, well, at least I didn't have to sell out to a greedy corporation to keep my head above water." Sean sidled past

Barry and mounted the stairs, returning to his perch halfway up. "You should be ashamed of yourself, packing those poor animals in like that with no room to move. The damned things aren't even healthy, and who knows what's in that feed the poultry company supply you with."

"I do what's necessary," Barry said, his tone acidic. "Your old man would've understood. He's probably turning in his grave at the thought of what you've done to his farm."

"You leave my dad out of this; God rest his soul." Sean bit his lip to stop himself from saying more. He needed this gig and could not afford to get fired. Speaking of which, Sean hadn't received a penny of the money he was owed for the job yet. He was almost finished and hadn't even been paid the deposit Barry had promised him a week ago to cover materials. Every time he had brought it up, there had been a new excuse, the latest being that Barry could not find the time to stop in at the bank. Sean probably should have refused to continue with the construction until he had the money, even if it was a handshake agreement, but work was not easy to come by and he didn't want to jeopardize his employment. Now though, he was almost finished and would be owed full payment by the end of the day. Barry, he noted, looked like he was about to leave, with a coat over his arm and car keys in hand. Sean realized he must broach the subject now or run the risk that he would have to return another day to get his money.

"I was hoping you see fit to settle up," Sean said. "I'll be done by day's end and could really use the money."

"I was wondering when you were going to bring that up." Barry reached into his pocket and produced a check, which he held out. "This will have to do. It's all I can afford."

Sean reached over the banister and took the check. He looked down, dismayed to see that it was several hundred pounds short. "What's this?"

"What does it look like?" Barry asked. "You wanted paying, I paid you."

"It's short." Sean could feel the anger building inside of him. Barry Clamagh was trying to stiff him. "This isn't the amount we agreed."

"No, but it's the amount I'm paying." Barry nodded toward the newly built staircase. "I'm not paying full price for shoddy work."

"My work's not shoddy." Sean clenched his fist, then unclenched it again. He took a step down the stairs toward Barry. "And you know it."

Barry backed up, the defiant look on his face replaced by one of concern. "You lay a finger on me and I'll have the sergeant up here."

"What, you think I'm going to waste my time beating on you?" The thought had crossed Sean's mind, but it was not worth it. He had no intention of spending a night in jail over Barry Clamagh. He forced his anger back down. "But you are going to pay up."

"Like hell I am." Barry nodded toward the check. "I'm not paying you a penny more than you already have."

"We had an agreement. You shook on it."

"Well now, did you bother to get that in writing?" The corners of Barry's lips lifted into a smirk.

"You know very well that I didn't."

"Maybe you should've." Barry's smirk widened. "Then you might have a leg to stand on. As it is, you'd do well to take what I'm willing to pay and be glad you got it."

"You'll regret this, Barry Clamagh." Sean's voice was trembling.

"I doubt it." Barry turned and opened the front door. As he stepped out, he glanced back over his shoulder toward Sean. "I take it you'll be done and out of my house by the time I get back."

"You can count on that," Sean said as Barry pulled the door closed. He stood there, on the stairs, hammer in hand, and looked at the check. There were still three stair treads to nail in place, but there was no way Sean was going to bother with that. He stepped down into the hallway and gathered his tools together, then closed the toolbox. In the kitchen, Lucy Clamagh was still on the phone, talking loudly and laughing, oblivious to her husband's mean-spirited shenanigans. Sean picked up his toolbox. Lucy may have to put up with Barry's ill temper and penny-pinching ways, but Sean did not. The bastard could finish the stairs himself. Sean was done.

TWENTY-FOUR

THE RIDE back to Clareconnell passed mostly in silence. If anyone had an idea regarding the whereabouts of Robert's body, they did not voice it. Their return to the surface had been met with relief by the sergeant, however when he noticed they were empty-handed his demeanor changed. Upon hearing that the body was missing, apparently dragged off by someone or something in the caves, his face turned ashen, but if he knew anything he would not say. Even when Hunt pressed him, Byrne refused to discuss the matter. Decker found this strange, but the sergeant seemed determined to escape further questioning, and when he received a phone call from Harry at the Claddagh, he excused himself and hurried to his vehicle, before following them back to the pub.

When they entered the Claddagh, Decker's attention was drawn to the bar where an attractive brunette in her late thirties was talking to Harry. She did not sound happy. As soon as she saw the sergeant enter, she left Harry and approached.

"I thought you would never get here." She looked distressed, Decker noticed, and her eyes were red as if she had been crying.

"What can I do for you, Ellen?" The sergeant stepped around the group and met her halfway. "Is everything all right?"

"No, everything is *not* all right." Ellen's voice teetered on the edge of hysteria. "Craig's missing. I thought maybe he went home with Sean after the pub last night, but Sean hasn't seen him since last call. He suggested I talk to Harry to see if there'd been a lock-in at the pub, but there wasn't. He left the pub ten minutes after Sean, but he didn't come home."

"Calm yourself, Ellen." The sergeant placed a reassuring hand on her shoulder. "I'm sure he'll show up. You know very well what Craig's like when he's been on a session. Boys will be boys."

"This is different. There's no one else he would go home with, other than Sean, and he isn't sleeping it off in one of Harry's rooms upstairs." Ellen looked up at the sergeant. "You have to help me find him. I'm worried something bad has happened."

"It's a small village. He can't have gone far." The sergeant gave her his best sympathetic look. "You should run on home now, Ellen. I'll ask around, see what I can turn up."

"How can I go home with my husband missing?" The sergeant's words were doing little to ease Ellen's fears.

"There's nothing else you *can* do, Ellen. Besides, you'll want to be there if Craig shows up." The sergeant steered her toward the door. "I'll let you know as soon as I find anything, I promise."

Ellen hesitated a moment, her eyes searching their faces for any sign of support. Then she hung her head, turned away, and left. The sergeant watched the door swing closed behind her, and Decker noted the look of concern that flashed across his face, but then the sergeant regained his composure. He rubbed his chin, stroking the stubble that grew there, and forced a weak smile.

"I'm sure there's nothing to worry about," he said, his nervous gaze shifting between Decker, Hunt, and the others. "Nothing to worry about at all."

TWENTY-FIVE

AFTER SERGEANT BYRNE and the still distraught Ellen Hennessey departed the Claddagh, the group stood in uneasy silence for a few seconds, before Colum spoke up, voicing what Decker suspected they were all thinking.

"I don't know about the rest of you, but I'm not finding the sergeant to be a particularly effective policeman."

"That suits me," Hunt said. "The last thing we want are the local authorities poking their nose into our business. I will say one thing though, he's acting mighty jumpy for a man whose job appears to entail nothing more than dealing with an occasional drunkard."

"When he's not in the pub right alongside the drunks," Colum said. "He'd had a skin full, to be sure, when he showed up at the monastery yesterday. I don't trust him either. He's a shifty one."

"I agree," Decker said. "I have a hunch there's something Sergeant Byrne isn't telling us. He actually looked scared to go down into the caves this morning."

"I think we'd do well to keep an eye on Byrne," Hunt said. He glanced at his watch. "But in the meantime, there's the matter of Astrid. The doctor said to give her twenty-four hours to recuperate and I think we have just about complied with that order. She should be awake by now. I think it's time we have a chat."

"Sounds like a fine plan to me." Colum turned toward the stairs.

"Hold on a minute." Hunt reached out and gripped the Irishman's arm. "Not so fast. I know you're concerned, which is most commendable, but I'd rather not have everyone traipsing in there. I'll go up with Rory. The two of you can stay down here, I'll fill you both in when I return."

"You're taking Rory with you?" Colum looked disappointed.

"Yes. He's the only other archaeologist we have on hand. I might need his assessment of the situation, depending upon what Astrid tells me. Have no fear, you'll get to see her soon enough."

"You're the boss." Colum shrugged, but his eyes drifted toward the stairs, anyway.

"Good man." Hunt nodded toward the bar. "Why don't you and John grab a pint."

"Don't you think it's a tad early for that?" Colum asked, surprised.

"Not at all, this is Ireland." Hunt started toward the stairs with Rory at his back. When he reached the door, he glanced over his shoulder. "Just don't get too carried away. We still have a missing body, and I'd like everyone reasonably sober should I need them."

Decker watched Hunt disappear up the stairs, then he turned to Colum. "I don't know about you, but I'm going to take Hunt up on his offer of a drink. Like the man said, this is Ireland, and even better, the boss is picking up the tab."

"Well now, when you put it like that..." Colum grinned and followed Decker to the bar where he ordered a pint of Guinness for each of them.

They settled on a pair of barstools and waited for their drinks. Decker was curious. "Just how long have you been working for Hunt?" he asked.

"A few years," Colum replied. "He recruited me right out of the Army. After twelve years with special forces I was looking for a change of pace."

"And you agreed to work for him, just like that?" Decker asked. "Didn't you have some concerns?"

"Hell, yes. I had a bucket load of them. I'd never even heard of CUSP. At first, I assumed they were just another private security firm. You know, one of those outfits that lease ex-soldiers like myself to the highest bidder. I had no interest in becoming a mercenary."

"And yet you signed on," Decker said as the pints arrived.

"They were very persuasive. Plus, they convinced me they had a higher mission. I was done playing soldier, and Hunt offered me a chance to do something different." Colum picked up his pint and took a long swig. He smacked his lips with pleasure. "Judging by your line of questioning, I assume you faced a similar moral crisis."

"I thought about Hunt's offer of employment long and hard," Decker admitted. "I ran into Hunt while I was in Alaska on a rather unusual freelance gig. He wasn't exactly open with me back then. In fact, he did what he could to obstruct my investigation at first. I have a feeling they only offered me a job because I know too much."

"Don't sell yourself short." Colum was already half done with his pint. "CUSP don't make job offers unless they see something in you."

"I guess I'm lucky then," Decker said. "Still, I didn't expect my first assignment to be running around an archaeological site."

"You'd be surprised where you end up in this job." Colum chuckled. "The things I've seen… I'll say this though, it's never boring."

"I assume you're not going to tell me any of those things you've seen."

"You assume correctly." Colum downed the last of his pint

and motioned for Harry to pour another. "One thing you learn in this job is to keep your mouth shut. They like to play it close to the chest."

"I'd noticed that." When Harry went to take Decker's pint, he put a hand over it and shook his head to decline the refill. "Speaking of playing things close, what do you think Hunt wants with Grendel's remains?"

"I have absolutely no idea," Colum said. "But this isn't the only archeological expedition CUSP has financed since I joined them. I know of at least three other digs around the world, including one in Greece, and another in Egypt."

"Do you think Hunt will tell us why Grendel's bones are so important?" Decker leaned on the bar. "It's hard to do a good job when you're not quite sure exactly what the job is."

"I wouldn't hold your breath." Colum glanced around as a pair of familiar figures appeared from the direction of stairs. "But we might at least find out what happened to Robert. It looks like the conversation with Astrid is over."

TWENTY-SIX

DECKER TURNED to see Hunt and Rory striding across the room in their direction. He could not help noticing the look on Hunt's face, a combination of annoyance and frustration.

If Colum noticed his boss's expression, he didn't show it. "Was Astrid awake?" He asked as they arrived at the bar. "What did she say?"

"She was awake," Hunt replied, his tone measured but tense.

"You found out what happened to Robert, then?"

"She gave an account of what went on in the caves." Hunt glanced between Decker and Colum. "I'm not sure I find it satisfactory."

"Why is that?" Decker asked. "You don't believe what she told you?"

"Disbelief is a strong word. Let's just say that there were some questionable decisions made – assuming her recollection of events is accurate."

"And?" Colum was growing impatient to hear what had transpired, and how Robert had died.

"Astrid says that it was Robert's idea to breach the crypt door and enter the labyrinth beyond, despite my explicit instructions to wait until we arrived before proceeding."

"That doesn't sound like Robert," Colum said. "On the few occasions I spoke to him, he came across as grounded and professional. Not the sort of chap to go off half-cocked or disobey direct orders."

"My sentiments exactly." Hunt folded his arms. "Regardless, we only have Astrid's version of events to go by, since Robert is not here to defend himself."

"Even if they went exploring without permission, that still doesn't explain how Robert ended up dead." Colum finished his pint and pushed the empty glass away.

"It was an accident, plain and simple, according to Astrid. She says that they entered the caves because Robert was excited about their discovery and didn't want to wait. He thought if he located the actual site of Grendel's burial, unearthed his remains, it would save time when we arrived."

"Except they didn't get that far," Decker said.

"No, they didn't. According to Astrid, they had barely gotten into the caves when Robert wandered too close to the edge of the chasm and fell. He was, apparently, still alive after the fall. She said he called out for help but there was no way down, so she ventured deeper into the caves, looking for a route to the underground river and the spot where Robert lay."

"She never found one, I assume," Colum remarked.

"No. She wandered for a while and then tried to find her way back to the cavern, but became lost when her flashlight batteries faded. She panicked and tripped in the darkness, hitting her head and losing consciousness. When she came around, the batteries had given out completely. After that, she stumbled around in the dark until she heard our voices and followed them to safety. She had no idea how long she was underground, or that Robert had died."

"That doesn't make sense," Colum said, a frown on his face. "It seems unlikely that Robert, an experienced archaeologist with many years of fieldwork under his belt, would be so careless. He would have known the dangers of venturing into unexplored cave systems and would have been careful regardless of his excitement."

"I agree," Rory said. "Robert excavated a cave site in France a few years ago. He'd also done extensive work excavating burial mounds in Sweden prior to joining this expedition. He knew what he was doing."

"Something else bothers me," Colum said. "You say Astrid claimed that Robert was still alive after the fall, that he called out for help?"

Hunt nodded. "That's what she told us."

"When I examined Robert's body, I didn't see any evidence that he survived the fall," Colum replied. "He was lying face down, and the loose gravel around his body wasn't disturbed. This would lead me to believe that he didn't move after impacting the ground. Of course, an autopsy will confirm if Robert was alive after he went over the edge, and for how long."

"Except that we don't have a body to perform an autopsy on," Decker observed. "And we have no idea where it went or how to locate it."

"Another reason I'm keeping an open mind regarding Astrid's testimony," Hunt said. "The sergeant was nowhere near as alarmed as he should've been over Robert's disappearance. In fact, he was more scared than concerned. There's something strange going on in this village, and I intend to find out what it is."

TWENTY-SEVEN

FATHER PATRICK CLEARY kneeled in the front pew of St. Ignatius Catholic Church with his head bowed in prayer. It was late in the evening, past ten o'clock, but the aging priest barely registered the passing of time. His earlier shock upon discovering the untouched body of Tom Walsh had given way to a festering unrest, and a dose of long overdue introspection. Never before had he questioned his role in the unusual ritual that had stripped the village of an actual burial for longer than anyone could remember. Clareconnell didn't even have a cemetery. There had never been a need for one. It had not escaped the priest that if Tom Walsh didn't go the way of every other village resident for hundreds of years, they would need one now.

Which was why he prayed.

He prayed that God would see fit to put things right. He prayed that whatever lurked in the tunnels beneath Clareconnell would remain there, as it had done for so many generations. Most importantly, he prayed for his eternal soul, because the priest wasn't entirely sure there was a place in heaven for him.

Father Cleary finished his prayer, his fingers working along the rosary beads clutched in one hand. He looked up, toward the crucifix high on the wall above the altar, and the tortured figure looking down upon him. If Jesus had died for man's sins, then the village of Clareconnell had surely contributed a larger share than most to their savior's anguish.

He pulled himself up, arthritic knees protesting the sudden movement, and sank back onto the church bench. It would do no good wallowing in self-pity. What was done, was done. He folded his arms against a sudden draft that whipped through the church. The priest looked around, wondering where the chill breeze had come from. Had someone entered? To his left several votive candles burned on a metal rack, their flames dancing back and forth. He cast a nervous glance over his shoulder toward the church doors, but they were closed. The pews were silent and empty. If someone had come in, they had not lingered. It would be odd for anyone to enter the church at this time of night, anyway. He left the doors unlocked all day for those who wished to stop in and pray, but normally secured them at night. The only reason he hadn't done so this evening was because he was in the church.

Father Cleary turned his attention back to the altar. His fingers found the small silver cross on his rosary beads. He clutched it in his palm and bowed his head once more to pray.

That was when he heard the noise.

It was barely audible, a light shuffle that would ordinarily not draw any attention. Tonight it did. The priest turned his head again and scanned the gloomy recesses of the church, his eyes searching every dark corner and unlit archway. As before, he saw nothing, and he wondered if he'd imagined the sound.

But then it came again.

A scuffing, dragging noise unlike anything he had encountered before.

The priest stood up, his eyes roaming the church as the first glimmers of panic set in. He couldn't see it, but he sensed the presence there with him, watching and biding its time.

"Who's there?" he called out, the hairs on his neck standing up as a tingle of apprehension coursed through him.

His only answer was a throaty grunt.

"Show yourself." The command came out weak and trembling. The priest stepped into the aisle with his back to the altar.

That was when he saw it.

A hunched shape at the back of the church. The lights in that area were off, but even so Father Cleary could make out the figure of a crouched man.

"What do you want?" Cleary took a step forward, then stopped, overcome with a sudden sense of dread. He could feel his heart thudding against his rib cage, so hard he feared it might crack his brittle bones. "Why are you here?"

The figure lifted its head, let out another guttural cough. It rose and stepped out of the shadows.

For the first time, the priest got a clear look at the figure, and what he saw made his blood run cold. This was no man, no parishioner stopping by on their way home from the pub to pray in front of their savior. This was a beast. It was tall. At least 6 feet, and maybe more. Its skin was brown and textured like old leather. Its head was enormous and grotesque, with heavy protruding eyebrows, sunken cheekbones, and a mouth that turned down at the corners. Tufts of flaxen blonde hair erupted from its cranium in splotches. Its hands, much too large, ended in elongated digits with thick yellowed nails, chipped and cracked in places. The beast was naked. Clearly male, it made no attempt to cover itself, but instead glared at the priest while flexing its rakish fingers open and closed. Worst of all were the creature's eyes. A dazzling blue, they shone with an intelligence unexpected in such a ghastly countenance.

Father Cleary let out a strangled whimper. He knew exactly what he was looking at, and where it had come from. Sometimes, in the dead of night, he would dream of coming face to face with the demon that inhabited the caves beneath Clareconnell, but upon waking the old man had always taken comfort because the beast could not escape. He now understood that he was wrong. Not only had the beast been freed, but somehow, impossibly, it was here in his church.

Cleary stumbled backwards, keeping his eyes fixed upon the monster that now advanced with slow, deliberate steps. He clutched the rosary beads tight; the crucifix digging into his palm and drawing blood that dripped to the floor as he retreated, leaving a trail of small crimson dots. His heel hit the altar steps. Too late, the priest realized where he was. He fought to remain upright but lost the battle. His rear end hit the steps, sending a flash of pain up his spine.

The creature closed in upon the stricken priest. Father Cleary, desperate to escape, scuttled backwards up the steps even as the beast closed in upon him.

"Get away from me," the priest cried in terror. "You shouldn't be here."

If the creature understood him, it didn't show it. Instead, it reached out and took hold of the priest by the lapels of his black jacket. It lifted him so that their eyes were level, and in that moment Father Cleary realized that he was in the grip of something truly evil, a fiend summoned from hell itself. He turned his head from the creature's fetid breath, and closed his eyes, lips moving in a silent prayer of attrition. The rosary beads fell from his hand.

The beast studied him for a moment, its mighty chest heaving. Father Cleary opened his eyes and met the monster's wide-eyed gaze, and for a moment he thought he might be spared, that the Lord had taken pity upon him. Until the beast pulled its lips back to reveal a mouth full of jagged yellow teeth, sharpened by years of gnawing on the bones of those unfortunate enough to cross his path. Then, as the beast lowered its head toward Father Cleary's exposed throat, the old priest realized that he wouldn't be spared. Because God had abandoned him, and because Grendel was hungry.

TWENTY-EIGHT

DECKER SAT at a corner table in the Claddagh Arms hunched over a pint of beer and ran through the day's events in his mind. On the table in front of him, open and facedown with the spine creased in half, was a tattered copy of Beowulf that Rory had provided under the guise of research. It was tough going, which was why Decker had abandoned the Old English poem in favor of a quiet pint and some introspection. Next to the book, laid out on the table, was a copy of the newly discovered text, known only to the few scholars associated with CUSP, that had led them to Ireland in the first place. This too was more than Decker's tired mind could wrap itself around at such a late hour. Still in the original dialect, he barely understood a word of the manuscript anyway. He would, he surmised, happily take Rory's word on the larger meaning of the text… Especially if it meant he didn't have to spend hours poring over it.

Besides, the story of Beowulf, while vaguely interesting, didn't seem to have much to do with current events in the village of Clareconnell. The dusty old stories were ancient history, assuming you believed anything contained within them. Decker was not sure that he did. The idea that a monster named Grendel had tormented the Danes every night for 12 years, during which time not a single warrior was able to vanquish the beast, was far-fetched. The arrival of the titular hero, Beowulf, raised its own questions, not least of which was the ease with which he dispatched Grendel when all others failed. That Beowulf then went on to also battle Grendel's mother and cut off her head, seemed equally implausible. The poem was, in Decker's opinion, nothing more than a fanciful myth. Yet Hunt and Rory believed that a real historical figure named Grendel was buried under the monastery, having used the second lesser-known text to guide them here.

Decker picked up the book and closed it, then glanced at his watch. It was after ten PM. He should probably finish his drink and head upstairs to bed. The rest of the group had already turned in for the night, and even though Decker's body clock was finally adjusting to the time difference, he knew that he would wake early in the morning, regardless. He lifted his pint to finish up and leave, but before he got that far, a woman with shoulder-length blonde hair and a trim figure entered the bar. Decker recognized her immediately. Astrid Hansen. The archaeologist who they had rescued from the caves the previous day.

She approached the bar and ordered a glass of red wine, then turned toward Decker and nodded toward the empty chair that sat opposite him.

"Are you alone?" She asked. Her voice was soft as silk, laced with the hint of an undefinable accent. "May I join you?"

"Be my guest," Decker said.

"Thank you." Astrid picked up her wine and crossed the bar, sinking down into the chair opposite him. "We haven't formally met. I'm Astrid Hansen."

"I know who you are." Decker finished the last of his pint and motioned to Harry for a refill. Now that Astrid was here, his desire to retire upstairs had diminished. He was curious about her and hoped to glean more information regarding Hunt's interest in Grendel. He also wondered if she would let slip any additional details concerning Robert's death and her subsequent ordeal in the caves.

"I know who you are, too." Astrid smiled, her deep blue eyes catching his. "You're John Decker. Adam Hunt's latest acquisition."

"I've never thought of myself as an acquisition before," Decker said with a laugh. "But it's as appropriate a description as any, I guess."

"Have you figured out why you're here yet?" Astrid sipped her wine, slender fingers holding the glass by the stem.

"I know we're looking for the remains of the mythical Grendel." Decker looked up as Harry brought him a fresh drink. He waited for the landlord to retreat, then spoke again. "If what I've been told is correct, his bones are buried under that monastery outside of the village."

"Grendel isn't a myth. He's as real as you or I. The Danes were so afraid of him they came all the way to Ireland and entombed him here." Astrid looked down at the copy of Beowulf and the reproduction of the lesser-known manuscript. "Those poems didn't get it completely right. The stories were passed down over so many generations they changed and morphed. At this point it's almost impossible to know the true history of what transpired back then, and exactly who the real Grendel was."

"Is that what you're doing here?" Decker asked. "Trying to sort out fact from fiction."

"Something like that." Astrid placed the wine glass on the table and ran a finger around the rim. "I've been searching for Grendel most of my life. You could say it's an obsession."

"One that you're on the edge of satisfying," Decker said. He wondered how old Astrid was. She possessed the confidence that normally came with age, yet she radiated an aura of vibrant youth. She was, he noted, stunning. Her face perfectly symmetrical, with flawless, milky-white skin. Her eyes shone with brilliant intensity. Her hair, perfectly styled, cascaded to her shoulders in a blonde waterfall, not a strand out of place. Decker would never have believed this woman was lost underground a mere 24 hours before. "It's a shame that tragedy struck when you were so near to the completion of your quest."

"Robert." Astrid hung her head. "I still can't believe he's dead. I begged him to wait, but he was gung-ho. All he wanted to do was find Grendel so there would be something to show Hunt when he arrived. I feel so guilty, getting lost in the caves like I did, instead of bringing help to him."

"It was an accident," Decker said, studying Astrid's face for any hint of deceit.

"A dreadful accident." Astrid wiped a tear from her cheek. "I should have been more forceful. Stopped him from going down there. If I had, he would still be alive."

"The right choice is easy to see in hindsight," Decker commented. "The hard thing is living with the consequences of our actions after the fact."

"So true." Astrid picked up her glass and finished the last of her wine. She sat in silence for a moment, then stood up. "It's late and I'm tired. I should be off to bed." She turned and placed the empty glass on the bar, then glanced back toward Decker, her eyes meeting his once again. When she spoke to him, her voice was soft and alluring. "Will you walk me to my room, Mr. Decker?"

"Sure." Decker pushed his chair back and stood up. He nodded farewell to Harry, who was wiping down the bar in slow lazy circles, and followed Astrid toward the stairs.

When they reached the top, Astrid paused. She turned toward Decker. "Thanks for sharing a drink with me this evening."

"My pleasure," Decker said. "I'm happy to talk anytime. Just come and find me."

"Thank you, I may do that. The last few days have been tough, and Adam Hunt all but implied I was lying about what happened at the monastery when we spoke earlier today. It's all rather upsetting, to tell the truth."

"Will you be okay tonight?"

"Yes, thanks to you." Astrid reached out and laid a gentle hand on Decker's arm. Her fingers lingered, the touch full of unrequited promise, and then she withdrew. "I'll see you tomorrow, Mr. Decker."

"Until then." Decker watched the alluring archaeologist retreat along the corridor toward her bedroom. He wasn't sure what had just happened, but in that moment when she touched him, he sensed an unspoken connection. He wondered if he was imagining things, or if Astrid Hansen had made a subtle pass at him. He was still pondering this, standing in the now empty corridor, when his phone rang. He took it from his pocket and looked down at the name on the screen. It was Nancy. Her unexpected call snapped him from his musings. He turned and headed toward his own room, answering as he went.

TWENTY-NINE

DECKER ENTERED his hotel room and closed the door. He sat on the bed and lifted the phone to his ear. "Hey."

"I thought you would have called before now," Nancy said. "You've been gone three days and I haven't heard a word since the night you arrived."

"Sorry, it's been busy here," Decker said. "Besides, I bet you're not even missing me. You've probably spent the last three days sitting around the pool drinking cocktails."

"I'm missing you, silly," Nancy replied. "But I know how much you hate lying by the pool. I have to admit, it's much less stressful when I don't feel you're bored all the time."

"Yeah. I'm not sure that sunbathing and sipping cocktails is really my thing. Still, I'm sorry I haven't called much." Decker wondered why he hadn't phoned except for one brief call the first night to let her know he'd arrived safely. Was it because she turned down his marriage proposal? He hadn't expected her to say no, and he felt hurt by the snub. After everything they'd gone through in Wolf Haven, and then during the hostage situation at the waterhole in Florida, he'd assumed she would be more than willing to be his wife. Now he wondered if Nancy was pulling away from him, or if she'd even ever really loved him. There would need to be a conversation regarding their relationship at some point, but he knew that now was not the time. Instead, he said: "I'll call more often, promise."

There was a moment of silence on the other end of the line, and then Nancy spoke again, clearly changing the subject. "How's Ireland, you found that pot of gold at the end of the rainbow yet?"

"Not so far," Decker said with a laugh. "But if I do, I'll let you know."

"Are you knee-deep in trouble as usual?"

"I don't know about that, but this assignment is certainly intriguing." Decker stood and went to the window. He looked out across the village and the dark skies beyond. "Not that I can say much about it. My new employer seems to value discretion."

"I bet Ireland is pretty." There was a pang of yearning in Nancy's voice. "I wish I was there with you."

"Me too." Decker's eyes settled upon the street below, his attention drawn by a movement in the darkness. He expected to see a villager, perhaps hurrying home from a night of drinking, but now that he looked closer, he saw nothing. The road was still and empty. Even so, he was sure there had been something there, slinking along in the shadows, but it was gone now, evaporating into the night like a ghost.

"You sound distracted," Nancy said. "I should let you go. It must be late there."

"It's almost midnight," Decker replied. "But it's always good to hear your voice."

"Yours too." A subtle sadness had replaced the yearning in Nancy's voice. "John…"

"Yes?"

Nancy paused, as if she wanted to say something but wasn't sure that she should. In the end she just said: "Never mind."

"Are you sure?" Decker asked. "You can always talk to me. You know that, right?"

"I know." Nancy hesitated before speaking again. "It can wait until your return. It's not important."

"If you're sure."

"I am. You just focus on the job at hand and come back to me safe and sound."

"That's the plan." Decker felt a tug of concern. Nancy's demeanor was doing little to convince him that she was invested in their relationship. He wondered if she wanted to discuss the marriage proposal as much as he did. Regardless, it would have to wait. He didn't want to push her, for fear of what she might say.

"Good night, John," Nancy said. "I love you."

"Love you too."

The line went dead. Nancy had hung up. Decker lingered at the window, his gaze returning to the spot where he'd seen the subtle, creeping movement, and felt a stirring of unease.

THIRTY

MOLLY WALSH, wife of the recently departed Tom Walsh, arrived at St. Ignatius Catholic Church not long after sunrise. Her husband had been dead only a few days, it was true, but that didn't mean she would shirk her duties. Cleaning the church had been a chore she was grateful to perform, for the parish and the Lord, for the past twenty years.

She stood outside the doors and waited for Gladys Peale to show up. Gladys, president of the local Women's Guild, had been cleaning the church even longer than Molly, and guarded her role as one of the few key holders with a zeal only matched by her attendance at mass seven days a week come rain or shine. Even the great blizzard that howled through in January of eighty-two, when Gladys was still a young woman, had not interrupted her devotions. Trudging through knee-high snow and cruel winds, she'd famously berated the priest of the time when she got there one frozen Wednesday morning to discover the church doors locked and the 7 AM mass canceled. Since then, Gladys had risen through the ranks of the Guild to become, arguably, the most influential woman in Clareconnell. Which was why, when Molly saw her bustling down the road fifteen minutes late for cleaning duties, she bit her lip.

"Good morning to you, Molly," Gladys said upon her arrival, her face creasing in sympathy. "How are you doing today, my dear?"

"As well as can be expected." She would be the focus of village sympathy, Molly realized, for a good while yet, even though she would rather people not feel compelled to mention the passing of her beloved husband every time they encountered her. Grief was hard enough without being constantly reminded of its cause. She fought back the lump that formed in her throat and turned toward the church doors. "We should get moving if we want the church spick and span before Father Cleary says mass."

Gladys shot her a look, and Molly realized that her innocent remark had been misconstrued as a passive aggressive jab regarding her coworker's tardiness. She considered apologizing and explaining that she had not meant the remark in a deroga-tory way, but changed her mind. Backpedaling would, most likely, only cement Gladys's view of her guilt. It was a no-win situation. She scolded herself and vowed to think before she opened her mouth in the future.

Gladys was pulling a key ring from her pocket now. She stepped up to the door and inserted the key into the lock, but then she frowned. "This isn't right. Is someone at the church already?"

"I don't think so," Molly said. "I haven't seen anyone this morning, and it's too early for Father Cleary to be up and about."

"Well then, why is the church unlocked already?" Gladys asked, perplexed. She pushed the door open. "Did you check it when you arrived?"

"No, why would I do that?" Molly shook her head. "It's always locked when I get here. You have the keys."

"It's not locked this morning." Gladys took a tentative step inside the church. Molly followed her in, noting how dark it was inside. The only illumination came from spotlights arranged near the altar. If anyone had entered before them, they had not turned on the rest of lights. "Do you think Father Cleary forgot to close up last night?"

"He never has before." Molly reached out and flicked the light switch. The sudden flood of illumination confirmed what she already knew. They were alone in the church.

"It's filthy in here." Gladys was staring down at the center aisle, where a set of muddy footprints led away toward the altar. "For heaven's sake, did someone forget to wipe their boots before they came in? That's just typical. I bet Barry Clamagh or one of his cronies from that disgusting chicken farm didn't bother to clean their wellies before they came lumbering in here. Some people have no respect. I don't know why Father Cleary puts up with it."

"Those don't look like they were left by boots," Molly commented, peering closely at the first set of footprints. "It looks more like whoever left these was barefoot. You can see the toe prints."

"Don't be daft." Gladys shook her head. "Why would anyone be walking around barefoot in the church?"

"I don't know, but they were." Molly stepped past her coworker and followed the muddy footprints down the aisle. When she reached the altar steps, she came to a halt, her eyes opening wide. "Gladys, come look at this."

"What is it now?" Gladys said, trudging up the aisle toward Molly. "Did they get dirt all over the altar too?"

"Not dirt." Molly was still staring at the steps, and the deep red stain that had spread across the polished wood floor and trickled down. Nearby lay a set of discarded rosary beads, the chain broken. Several loose beads had rolled into the congealed goo and gotten stuck. "I don't know what this is."

Gladys looked down in disbelief. "Oh dear. That's not right. Not right at all."

"I think we should call Aiden Byrne," Molly said, her voice trembling, because she now realized what she was looking at. "That's blood. A whole lot of it."

THIRTY-ONE

ON HIS THIRD morning in Ireland, Decker rose early and went for a walk. He hadn't truly explored the village yet and was curious to get the lay of the land. He left the Claddagh and walked down Winslow Road toward the local church, a stone building with a square tower. Along the way he passed a row of terraced homes with front doors painted in bright colors. Red and blue. Green and yellow. On the other side, shops and a supermarket were dotted between the cottages. At the church doors, two women stood chatting. They ignored him and he kept going. When he looked around again, they were gone. It didn't take long for the homes and shops to peter out, giving way to rugged scrubland and fields, so Decker veered off and took a side road. There were more houses here, cute whitewashed cottages with slate roofs. Some were in better repair than others, a sign of the economic hardships of village life. He wondered what the occupants did for work. Some, he guessed, worked on nearby farms. He could see the farmhouses poking up out of the rolling landscape, their stone edifices breaking the patchwork quilt of fields that fell away to the horizon. Other people surely worked in the village, employed by the shops that lined the main street. He followed the road as it curved back around behind the pub, crossing over a stone bridge under which a stream gurgled. Eventually he found himself at the opposite end of the village and started back in the other direction. As he walked, he reflected upon the reason he was here, and his new employer. So far, he felt underutilized. He could not see why Hunt wanted him along on this trip. He was a trained policeman and had assumed that he was being employed to fulfill that role. All he'd done up to this point was ride around in the Land Rover, trudge through a few chilly caves, and sit in the bar drinking Guinness. Hunt had barely consulted him on anything, even sidelining him when Astrid had awoken. He wondered if he'd made the right choice signing up with CUSP.

He strolled back down Winslow Road and was soon at the Claddagh again. He stopped outside for a moment and glanced around. Something was nagging at him regarding his walk through the village but he couldn't put his finger on it. He wondered if it was related to his sense of unease the previous night when he was standing at the bedroom window after Nancy hung up. He gazed across the road toward the area where he'd seen movement in the darkness, but it jogged nothing loose. Pushing the errant thought away, Decker turned, pulled the pub door open and stepped inside.

His colleagues were already seated for breakfast at their usual table when he entered. Today, though, Astrid had joined them for the first time. As he approached, Colum looked up with a toothy grin.

"Where the blazes have you been?" The Irishman asked. "No one else will give me their black pudding."

"I went for a stroll," Decker replied, motioning to Harry and ordering breakfast before speaking again. "I wanted to get a look at the village. Since we all agree that Sergeant Byrne has been acting oddly ever since Robert's body disappeared, I thought it would be prudent to scout around a little. It's always helpful to know your surroundings."

"Was it useful?" Hunt took a slice of toast from the rack in the center of the table and buttered it.

"I'm not sure," Decker admitted, as his breakfast arrived in record time—full Irish as usual. He waited while Colum helped himself to the puddings, then tucked in, talking between mouthfuls. "The village is quiet. I saw nothing that would raise my suspicions that the sergeant is keeping secrets from us."

"Speaking of Robert, Astrid would like to go back to the caves today." Hunt chewed his toast and swallowed before talking again. "She also wants to retrieve the artifacts recovered prior to the accident. She doesn't think it's a good idea to leave them up there if no one is working on the dig."

"I agree with that," Rory said. "From what she's been telling me, they made some pretty exciting finds."

"Really? Like what?" Decker asked. He wasn't sure he was really that interested in the archeological side of things, but it seemed like the right question to ask. Besides, his intuition told him that there was something not quite right about the village, and it would be foolhardy not to gather as much information as possible.

"Well, Danish relics for a start. Items that should not be at a monastery in Ireland."

"The Danes came to Ireland several times," Rory added. "And we know from our alternative manuscript that they came to this area with the express purpose of burying Grendel. If what Astrid says is true, it would indicate that they also set up a settlement here."

"Not a large one, to be sure," Astrid said. "Our research indicates it would have been a very small contingent of men, probably warriors, that remained here."

"And you know this because of the artifacts you found?" Decker asked.

"Exactly." Astrid nodded. "Whoever these men were, they never left. My theory is that they intermingled with the locals and their offspring became absorbed into the general populace over the generations."

"I'd love to run DNA testing on the villagers to determine their ancestry." Rory was talking faster as the conversation progressed, overwhelmed by excitement. "But it's unlikely I will get permission to do it."

"Your assumption is correct." Hunt looked up from his food. "Have you forgotten that we're trying to remain low-profile here? Swabbing the locals to run tests on them will make it hard to maintain the cover story that we're from UNESCO."

"Shame." Rory looked disappointed. "We have the Danish artifacts though. The sooner we get to the monastery and retrieve them, the better."

"I agree." Hunt tapped his mouth with a napkin and then stood up. "I suggest that we take a few minutes to get ready and then meet Colum at the car."

The group dispersed, heading for the stairs. As Hunt prepared to follow, Decker reached out a hand and stopped him. A nagging had been flitting at the edges of his mind regarding the village, and now he realized why. "I need to tell you something."

Hunt raised an eyebrow. "I'm all ears."

"I don't know if this is relevant, but I just realized something regarding my walk through the village." Decker glanced around the room, but they were the only people there. He could hear Harry clattering around in the kitchen. "The people of Clareconnell have nowhere to bury their dead. I walked a loop around the entire place and I never found a cemetery."

"You're sure about that?" Hunt asked, his eyes narrowing.

"I'm sure," Decker said. "I don't know how that fits in with anything else that's going on, but it's odd."

"It is indeed." Hunt paused as if thinking. "I'm getting a bad feeling about this village, and my hunches are rarely wrong."

THIRTY-TWO

SERGEANT BYRNE WAS TAKING his morning shower when he heard the phone ring. He cursed and shut the water off, grabbed a towel, wrapped it around himself and hurried into the bedroom where his phone sat on the nightstand. He scooped it up and answered, hoping that whatever minor emergency had pulled him from his hot shower would be easily solved, allowing him to return. He did not expect to hear the voice of Gladys Peale, a woman he barely tolerated on the best of days, screeching down the phone at him in an unintelligible jumble of mashed together words.

"Gladys, speak slower," Byrne said over the still gabbing woman, injecting as much authority into his voice as he could muster. "I can't understand a word you're saying."

This didn't help, in fact it seemed to encourage the panicked woman to talk even faster. He pulled the phone away from his ear and switched over to speaker. At least this way he wasn't damaging his eardrums.

"For the love of God, Gladys, take a breath."

If Gladys took his advice, he never found out. A new voice took over, which he recognized as Molly Walsh.

"I'm at St. Ignatius. There's blood all over the church." Molly sounded no less distressed, but at least she had the good sense to keep her hysteria under control long enough to convey the reason for their panic. "The altar's covered in it, and we found more near the back of the church, by the doors."

"You're sure it's blood?" Byrne asked. He abandoned the towel on the bed and went to his wardrobe, and pulled out a clean shirt and pants. He could hear the shower running in the next room, but he wouldn't be relaxing under it again anytime soon.

"I'm not sure, no." Molly's exasperation was clear even through the phone's speaker. "But it looks like blood, and I can't imagine what else it could be. Besides, Father Cleary is nowhere to be found. He isn't at the Presbytery and he's not answering the phone. I'm worried something has happened. His rosary is here, all broken up, as if it were ripped out of his hands."

"Give me five minutes," he said, pulling the shirt on and buttoning it up. "Stay where you are and don't touch anything."

"We'll wait for you outside," Molly said. "I can't stand to look at it a moment longer."

"That's probably for the best, anyway." Byrne was buttoning his pants. "Don't let anyone in before I get there."

He hung up, finished dressing, and turned off the shower. He hurried through the house and out to his car. Five minutes later he was pulling up outside of St. Ignatius.

Molly and Gladys were waiting outside. They hurried toward the car when they saw him, the relief on their faces clear. They all but dragged him up the path toward the church doors, but when they got there they stopped, clearly fearful of reentering the church.

"I think you ladies should stay out here while I investigate," Byrne said, noting their reticence.

He opened the door and peered into the dim space beyond. At first, he saw nothing out of place, but then his eyes picked out the muddy footprints that led along the center aisle. He might only be a small village Garda, but he knew evidence when he saw it. Not that it hadn't already been tainted. The two women had apparently trudged around the church before they noticed anything amiss. If a crime had been committed, he would be forced to call in a crime scene examiner from Dublin. That was not a pleasant thought. The village had spent years keeping to itself, and the last thing they needed was national attention.

Sergeant Byrne pulled on a pair of latex gloves, and slipped into the church. He pushed the doors closed behind him, depriving the still nervous but inquisitive women of their view. He glanced around before proceeding, noting several crimson drips on the floor near the doors. It was pure luck, he realized, that Molly and Gladys had not stepped on these when they originally entered the church, oblivious to their presence. Now he stepped tentatively around them and took a circuitous route to the altar, avoiding the main aisle. When he reached the front of the church he came to a halt, unable to contain an involuntary shudder.

There was blood here, to be sure.

Lots of it.

Sergeant Byrne took a moment to gather his wits and then, without taking another step, scanned the rest of the church. Nothing else looked out of place, and there was no sign that a robbery had occurred. He also noted the lack of a source for the blood. That it came from Father Cleary seemed self-evident given the broken and abandoned rosary beads nearby, but of the priest himself there was no sign. This did not mean a crime had occurred, Byrne thought to himself. For all he knew, the priest might have cut himself or had some other accident and was right now on his way to the hospital in Kilkenny. This would also explain the church doors being unlocked when the cleaners had arrived. If Father Cleary had left in a hurry, he might very well have neglected to lock up. This did not, however, explain the muddy footprints which looked like they had been made by a barefooted individual.

Sergeant Byrne felt stirrings of unease. He took out his cell phone and even though the cleaners had already tried this, made a call to Father Cleary's cell phone. No answer. It rang once and went to voicemail. Next, he tried the Presbytery landline with the same luck. This didn't rule out an accident having befallen the priest, but it didn't bode well even so. He would check in with Doctor Winslow and the hospital in Kilkenny as soon as he was done here, but there was something else he wanted to check first.

Sergeant Byrne skirted the pool of congealed blood and made his way to the door next to the lady chapel. He entered and hurried down below the church. He flicked the lights on and all but jogged down the tunnel toward the room where they had laid Tom Walsh forty-eight hours before. When he arrived, the door was closed and bolted. He pressed his eye to the peephole, which confirmed his suspicion. Uncoiling the rope from its cleat, he dropped the sturdy inner door back into place and drew back the bolts flinging the outer door wide. Tom Walsh lay undisturbed, his face looking as unhappy in death as he had been happy in life. His eyes bulged wide. His tongue poked through anemic lips as if he were making an obscene gesture toward the repulsed policeman. The unembalmed corpse was taking on a dull green hue.

Sergeant Byrne leaned heavily against the doorframe. When he called around to locate the parish priest he would get nowhere, he was sure. This wasn't the first person who had gone missing over the past couple of days in Clareconnell. The one person who should have been missing, Tom Walsh, was not. This led him to an inescapable conclusion. The beast with whom the village had sustained an uneasy harmony for so long was not interested in the dead meat they provided for it any longer. Not only that, it was no longer in the labyrinth but had been freed to wreak havoc upon anyone who crossed its path. There was only one way that could have happened.

The archaeologists at the monastery.

Sergeant Byrne turned and hurried back along the corridor

without bothering to open the inner door to the caves again. There was no point now. The beast would not take Tom Walsh. He took the steps back up to the church two at a time and hurried toward the main doors. When he exited, Gladys and Molly were still there, lingering at the entrance.

"Keys," he said to Gladys. "Now."

She hesitated, reluctant to relinquish them, and by association, her responsibility.

"Come on, woman, I don't have time for this." Byrne snapped, barely able to conceal his dislike for the town busybody.

"You don't need to be curt, Sergeant Byrne." Gladys held the keys out.

He snatched them and locked the church doors. The last thing he needed was the cleaners going back inside and wrecking his scene, or worse, Molly going under the church and seeing her husband's unsightly body. Then he pocketed the keys and sprinted to his car, taking out his phone and placing a call to the Claddagh Arms as he went. With any luck those people from UNESCO were still there, and he wanted to make sure they stayed that way, at least for a while. That done, he pocketed the phone and pulled the car door open. As he was about to climb in, he noticed Sean O'Mara walking along the road toward him. This was perfect. He stepped in Sean's path; arms raised to draw his attention. Moments later, arrangements made, Aiden Byrne was speeding toward the monastery ruins.

THIRTY-THREE

SEAN O'MARA HADN'T HEARD from Craig since leaving the Claddagh two evenings before. He'd called him several times and left a couple of messages already without a response. He was now getting worried, so since he had to go into town and deposit Barry Clamagh's check anyway, he decided to stop by the house and see if Craig was there. The bank opened at nine. By ten past he was on Craig Hennessy's doorstep.

Ellen answered.

She looked tired, her eyes puffy and red. He wondered if she'd been crying. This did not bode well for Craig having shown up.

"How are you, Ellen?" Sean asked, even though her gaunt face had already answered the question.

"I've been better." Ellen sniffed and hugged her arms across her chest. "I haven't seen Craig in two days. I don't know what to do."

"You've talked to Sergeant Byrne, I imagine."

"I spoke to him yesterday and haven't heard a thing since," Ellen said. "That feckin useless gobshite couldn't find a priest in a seminary."

"You don't think he found out about..." Sean let the words trail off.

"Heavens, no." Ellen glanced up and down the street. "If you're going to bring that up, you'd better come in."

Sean stepped past Ellen and into the house. After she closed the door, he spoke again. "I don't like bringing it up, I know it's in the past, but we have to consider that Craig might have found out."

"What happened was a mistake, Sean." Ellen walked past him toward the kitchen. "You want a cup of tea?"

"No, thank you." Sean tagged along behind her. He leaned in the kitchen doorway and watched as she fussed around, pulling tea bags from the cupboard, putting the kettle on the stove. "Mistake or not, it happened."

Ellen turned to him; her eyes wide. "It was one night. That's all. You know what it's been like for Craig and me these past few years. When we had that fight, when he walked out, I made a stupid mistake. I called you because I had no one else. I let things go too far. It was a lapse in judgment, and it should never have happened. Christ, you're Craig's best friend for pity's sake. What was I thinking?"

"You were acting on your true feelings," Sean said. "We both were."

"There are no feelings. I was vulnerable and upset, nothing more."

"You know that's not true."

"It doesn't matter. I'm married to Craig. This isn't about that. When Craig left that night after we fought, he went to the Claddagh. I knew where he was. This time it's different. He never came home from the pub. For Pete's sake, you were with him all day and night. Don't you think he would've said so if he knew what we'd done?"

"I don't know." Sean entered the kitchen. He placed a hand on Ellen's shoulder and pulled her close. "What other explanation could there be?"

127

"I have no idea." Ellen rested her head on his shoulder. Tears wet his shirt. "I'm so scared and no one's helping me. I might not love Craig like I did when I married him, but I don't want this."

"We'll find him." Sean lifted her head, so she was looking at him. "One way or the other, we'll find him."

"How?" Ellen wiped the tears from her cheeks. "He's not answering his phone. No one's seen him for days. Not even Harry. It's like he just fell off the earth. Sergeant Byrne won't even take me seriously. I can't imagine what people are saying behind my back."

"No one saying anything, Ellen." Sean stepped away. "There's only a few people that know you and Craig were even having problems."

"You should go." Ellen nodded toward the door. "It's bad enough that Craig's missing, I don't want tongues wagging about the two of us on top of it."

"Ellen…"

"I mean it, Sean." Ellen bustled him back down the hallway toward the front door. "I appreciate you coming around, but this isn't helping."

Sean nodded. He stepped outside and then, once he was on the stoop, he turned back to her. "I'll drop by again in a few days and see how you are, okay?"

Ellen nodded but said nothing. She retreated and closed the front door, leaving Sean alone on the doorstep. He stood there a moment, gathering his thoughts, and then took off back toward town. He strolled down Winslow Road, disturbed by the prolonged absence of his friend. It wasn't like Craig to go missing, and Ellen was probably right when she said that his disappearance had nothing to do with their brief and ill-advised liaison. The affair, if you could even call it that, was two years in the past. If Craig knew about it, he'd kept quiet. The more he thought about it, the more Sean came to the conclusion that this was different. Craig had been talking about leaving the village and going to Dublin, but he never mentioned doing it alone. Besides, Sean knew it was nothing but idle talk, and nothing his friend intended to follow through with in such a brief span of time. Also, it wasn't like Craig had moved out. His clothes and other possessions were, presumably, still there, as was his car, which was parked at the curb outside the house. Wherever Craig had gone, he went there on foot.

Sean was still pondering this, running scenarios through his mind, when he came upon St. Ignatius church, and an odd scene. Molly Walsh and Gladys Peale lingering near the church doors with concerned looks on their faces, and Sergeant Byrne standing in the road, waving him down.

THIRTY-FOUR

WHEN DECKER ENTERED the Claddagh Arms parking lot, he found Hunt and the others standing in a loose semicircle around Colum, who was on his knees next to the vehicle's rear wheel.

"What's going on?" He asked, approaching the group.

"Flat tire," Colum growled as he struggled to remove the wheel nuts with a lug wrench. "I can't imagine how this happened. It was fine when we parked yesterday, and now there's a cut in the tire. If I didn't know better, I'd say it was done on purpose."

Decker exchanged a glance with Hunt. It was just one more strange occurrence to add to a growing list. He glanced around the parking lot. "What about the rental car Robert and Astrid were using? Can't we take that?"

"It's gone," Hunt replied. "It was in Robert's name. Our European Field Office had the rental company pick it up earlier this morning."

"That's too bad," Decker said. "Anything I can do to help?"

"Not unless you know how to patch a tire," Colum said. "Have no fear, I'll be finished before you know it."

Despite Colum's proclamation, it took an additional thirty

minutes to mount the spare wheel, at which point they piled into the Land Rover with Hunt in the front passenger seat, and Decker sandwiched between Astrid and Rory in the back. As soon as they were settled, Colum started the engine and pulled out onto Winslow Street, glowering at the thought of finding somewhere to replace the damaged tire, which he claimed would be easier said than done in the village. He would have to drive to Kilkenny, he grumbled, to find a mechanic with the correct radius in stock.

As they left the village behind it started to rain, a steady drizzle too heavy for the intermittent wipers, but not heavy enough to keep the wipers on continuously. This was why they were almost upon it by the time they saw Clareconnell's only Garda cruiser speeding in the other direction toward the village. At the wheel was Sergeant Byrne. Next to him in the passenger seat Decker saw another man, but he could not make out his features through the rain.

"I wonder what the sergeant was up to?" Hunt said. "It looks like he was coming from the direction of the monastery."

"Do you think he was looking for Robert's body?" Astrid asked, turning to look through the rear window as the police car receded into the distance. "Do you think he found it?"

"I doubt it," Decker said. "There's no sign of a vehicle to transport the body, and Sergeant Byrne was reluctant to even step foot in the caves yesterday. Whatever he was doing, I'm sure it had nothing to do with Robert."

"We'll find out soon enough," Colum said as they turned onto the trail leading to the monastery and pulled up next to the ruin.

They piled out, bowing their heads against the rain, and hurried towards the dig site and the steps leading beneath the monastery. When they arrived Astrid noticed that something was awry immediately. She ran toward the tent under which the artifacts were stored, a look of horror on her face.

"Everything's gone." She looked around as if she expected to see the crates of relics in another location. "Everything we discovered was here. Byrne must have taken it all. He's cleaned us out. Why would he do this?"

"I knew we shouldn't have left it here." Rory looked glum. "I hadn't even had time to inspect the finds yet."

"Maybe he took them for safekeeping," Hunt said, but he didn't sound convinced.

"Not likely," Decker said. "He doesn't strike me as the considerate kind. There's something else going on here."

"Come along." Hunt approached the crypt entrance. "I want to make sure there's nothing amiss down below."

Astrid turned her attention from the missing artifacts and joined Hunt. Colum stepped down into the hole and followed the winding stairs downward, taking it slow and steady. Decker went next, descending into the darkness. At the bottom he waited for the others to descend, and then they hurried to the inner chamber and the door carved with demons. But when they got there, a shocking discovery awaited them.

"Now we know what he was doing here," Colum said, pulling on a sturdy padlock that had been attached to the door. A notice next to it declaring the caves beyond to be a crime scene.

"This doesn't make sense," Astrid said, a tremble of panic in her voice. "We've had no problems with the local authorities. We have permits and permission to be here. He can't do this."

"Tell that to him," Decker said.

"I need to get into those caves." There was frustration in Astrid's voice. And something else too. Anger. "There are more artifacts. Important discoveries that need to be brought to the surface and examined. Robert is in there too. We have to find him."

"I agree," Hunt said through tight lips. "But we're not getting in there anytime soon. Our best bet is to go back to the village and find out why the sergeant has done this."

"Maybe it has something to do with whatever dragged

Robert off," Colum said. "There's no other reason to lock the caves."

"No, there isn't," Hunt agreed.

"Sergeant Byrne has been holding out on us ever since we discovered Robert's body. He already knows what dragged Robert off, I'll wager." Decker turned away from the door. "And he's afraid of it. In fact, I'd go as far as saying he's terrified…"

THIRTY-FIVE

COLUM DROVE DIRECTLY to the Garda station and came to a screeching halt outside. He'd barely stopped before Hunt was jumping out of the Land Rover and slamming the door behind him. Decker exited and followed Hunt as he flung open the door to the Garda station and stepped inside.

"Why the hell are the caves locked?" Hunt asked without waiting for the startled policeman to realize what was going on.

"I gather you've been to the monastery then?" Sergeant Byrne was sitting in the larger of the converted cottage's two downstairs rooms, behind a worn desk that could use a fresh coat of varnish. The other room, Decker noted, contained two small cells, which was probably one more than the village needed. Today they were both empty.

"We have permission from Dublin to be up at that monastery." Hunt was seething. Decker could see the veins standing out on the sides of his neck. "You have no right to deny us access."

"I can do whatever I want." The sergeant leaned back in his chair and smiled. "This is my village and I have the final say what goes on here."

"We still have a man missing in those caves, or did you forget that?" Hunt crossed to the desk and leaned close to the sergeant. "Don't make me go over your head."

"I'm well-aware that your archaeologist is missing. That's precisely why I don't want people down there. You've already confirmed that he's dead, so finding him is nothing more than a retrieval operation at this point. There's nothing you can do to help the man. I do, however, want to make sure there are no more accidents." Byrne met Hunt's gaze with cool indifference. The look on his face betrayed the fact that he was enjoying the control he felt he now had. "As for going over my head, you're with UNESCO, not Interpol. You don't exactly have much leverage."

"You don't want to get in my way," Hunt said through gritted teeth.

Decker stepped forward, sensing that the situation was about to get out of control. He took Hunt's arm and steered him from the desk. In the doorway behind them Rory, Colum, and Astrid stood mutely watching the scene play out. "Let me handle this," Decker said. He turned to the sergeant and spoke in a calm voice. "We want to find our man. Just give us some time in the caves so we can do that. You can accompany us if you'd like."

"No one is going back under the monastery." Sergeant Byrne was unmovable. "Not you, not cave rescue, and certainly not me."

"What are you afraid of?" From his rear, Decker heard Hunt breathing heavily. The man did not like people getting in his way.

"I'm not afraid of anything," Byrne replied, although the way he avoided Decker's gaze when he spoke revealed his lie.

"You know what's in those caves, don't you?"

"I know that they're dangerous. I know that you people shouldn't have been poking around them in the first place." Byrne pushed his chair back and stood up, raising himself to his full height. "The caves under the monastery stay sealed until I decide otherwise. I don't care which organization you're from, or what permits you have. I make the rules in this village and until I'm instructed otherwise by my Inspector, that entire area is off limits. None of you are to go anywhere near the monastery, and if I catch you up there, I'll arrest you."

"What about the artifacts we found?" Astrid pushed her way forward. "I know you took them."

"I retrieved objects of cultural significance that had been carelessly abandoned. I don't know what kind of operation you were running up there, but if you ask me, it was sloppy."

"Now look here—"

"Let it be." Decker stepped between her and Sergeant Byrne. "It's not worth it. This isn't achieving anything."

"You should listen to him," Byrne nodded in Decker's direction. "He appears to be the only one who understands your situation."

"All I understand is your obstructing us for no good reason," Decker said. "And you still have not provided a satisfactory answer to my question."

"I don't need to answer your question." Byrne folded his arms. "But I do need you to leave my office. This conversation is over."

Decker observed the other man for a moment, gauging his resolve. Then he turned to Hunt and the rest of the group. "I think it's time we left. We're wasting our time here."

Hunt glared past Decker toward the sergeant, but he kept quiet, no doubt aware that Decker was correct. Then he turned and stomped out of the Garda station. Decker and the others filed out after him.

As they departed, Byrne gave them one last warning. "And remember, stay away from that monastery. Otherwise you'll leave me no choice but to throw you all in the cells."

THIRTY-SIX

SERGEANT BYRNE WATCHED Adam Hunt and the group from UNESCO depart. He didn't believe for one moment that they were with the United Nations in any capacity. The way Hunt carried himself, with an air of confident authority, would suggest another, less mundane, organization. Sergeant Byrne had no idea who that group might be, but while they were maintaining their cover story, they would not invoke a higher authority. Of that he was sure. The bigger question was their true purpose in Clareconnell. Nobody cared enough about the monastery to declare it a world heritage site. The ancient building was falling into the ground. There were hundreds of old churches and monasteries in Ireland, many of them in much better condition. Was it possible that they knew the village's secret? He doubted it. Otherwise there wouldn't have been a dead archaeologist in the caves. The outsiders were oblivious to the beast that dwelt in the labyrinth beneath their feet. That didn't mean they would stay that way. They were after something, and whatever it was required access to the caves. Someone had created an elaborate cover story to hide their true intentions, a story that had fooled the authorities in Dublin into issuing the dig permits. That suggested a degree of sophistication. He would need to be careful.

Locking the caves and denying the fake UNESCO group access had been a good start. If he was correct, it had also taken care of their other situation. The beast had gotten loose when the archaeologists opened the caves, and now two people were missing, presumably dead. The one thing that both incidents had in common was that they appeared to have taken place at night which meant that the beast was probably not comfortable out in the open during daylight. It would retreat to the place where it felt safest. The caves under Clareconnell. Now that the door was secure again, the beast was once more trapped. The status quo had been restored.

Except that he didn't trust the outsiders to obey his orders. He couldn't force them out of the village, and he harbored little hope that they would depart of their own free will, especially when one of their own, albeit deceased, was missing. That meant he would need to keep an eye on them. Sergeant Byrne went to the window. The Land Rover carrying the fake UNESCO group was turning back into the Claddagh Arms parking lot. He watched it disappear from view around the side of the building before turning back to his desk and sitting down once more. Then he picked up his phone and called Harry the landlord for the second time that day.

THIRTY-SEVEN

AN HOUR after the confrontation with Sergeant Byrne at the Garda station, Adam Hunt was still steaming. The group was gathered around a table in the bar at the Claddagh Arms discussing their next move.

"One phone call back to the States, that's all it would take to bring that moronic cretin to heel." Hunt took a deep breath. "He's lucky I want to maintain our cover here or Sergeant Byrne would find himself out of a job in ten seconds flat. He has no idea who he's dealing with."

"The hell with him," Colum said before standing and going to the bar where he ordered a pint. Upon returning, he settled back into his seat and looked around the group. "I say we go up there right now and smash that lock off. Robert's in those caves somewhere and it's not right that he's keeping us from finding him."

"Easy there," Hunt said. "No one is doing anything stupid. The sergeant said that we stay away from the monastery and that's what I intend to do… for now."

"And what about the stuff he confiscated?" Astrid spoke up. "The artifacts we recovered during our dig. The permits give us custody of anything we find until the Irish government says otherwise. He has no right to take them."

"No, he doesn't." Hunt's voice had returned to a more even cadence now, but Decker could tell that he was still mad. The anger danced behind his eyes, but Hunt, ever the professional, had reined it in. "It will do us no good to go at this thing with a sledgehammer. Sergeant Byrne makes the rules around here, or so it would appear. We need to approach this problem with a little more finesse."

"What have you got in mind?" Decker asked. He recognized the sergeant's small-minded, small town attitude. He'd seen it before. Give a man a lick of power and see where he takes it. Some, the good cops, used it with compassion and fairness. Others, like the sergeant, ended up bloated with self-importance and high on their own authority. It was strange that more often than not, those who abused their power the most, were also most inept.

"I'd rather not discuss that just yet," Hunt said. "I'll let you know when I deem it necessary."

"Speaking of necessary information," Decker said. "It's still not clear to me why we are here."

"To retrieve the bones of Grendel," Rory said as he sipped a finger of Jamison's. "We went over all this on the flight here."

"It's true that you told me we were retrieving Grendel's bones." Decker looked at Hunt. "But that's pretty much all you told me. You never said why you want the bones. I can't for the life of me see any practical application that CUSP could have for such a thing. If we worked for a museum, or a university, that would be different, but we don't."

"Again, need to know," Hunt replied.

"A man has died over this already. I think we need to know." Decker knew he was on thin ice pressing the matter. He was a new employee and had no standing to demand anything. He didn't enjoy working in the dark though, especially when he felt like pertinent information was being withheld for the sake of it. "What harm can it do to tell us?"

"Maybe you're right." Hunt shrugged. "Many of our expeditions and projects have national security implications, but in this case there are no such concerns. Our interest skews more toward the scientific."

"And?" Decker leaned forward.

"How's your knowledge of the Bible, Mr. Decker?" Hunt asked.

"I'd say it's average," Decker said. He'd attended church with his mother when he was a child, but later, after her death, it all changed. He wasn't sure if his father ever truly believed, or if the death of his wife stripped him of his faith. Either way neither of the Decker men set foot in a house of God after that. Now he struggled to remember much of the information imparted to him during Bible study all those years ago.

"I assume that you've heard of Cain, who murdered his brother Abel," Hunt asked.

"Sure." Decker nodded. "Weren't they the sons of Adam and Eve?"

"Very good." The corners of Hunt's mouth turned up into a slight smile. "After Cain committed his heinous crime, God banished him from the garden of Eden into a life of wandering as punishment for his sins. Tradition states that Cain had an unnaturally long lifespan, dying in Noah's flood after fathering many children."

"I don't see what this has to do with Grendel," Decker said, furrowing his brow.

"It's simple," Rory said, taking over. "Grendel and his mother are both direct descendants of Cain, at least if you believe the original text. According to legend, they were just as long-lived as their ancestor, and possessed magic powers to boot."

"This sounds like a half-baked fantasy." Decker could accept that the Beowulf text might have originated with real people and actual events that had become distorted over time. A case of centuries-long Chinese whispers, the story changing and becoming more embellished each time it was told. What he found hard to believe was that Cain and Abel were real and that Cain fathered a lineage that ended with a historical Grendel who genuinely possessed the traits attributed to him in the ancient poem.

"There's nothing fantastical to it," Astrid said. "Grendel and his mother were quite real, I assure you. The Danes really did bring him here. He's in those caves, under the monastery as we speak."

"Okay, let's say I believe you. I still don't have an answer to my question." Decker looked around the group. "What's so important about the remains of Grendel that we're willing to defy the local authorities to get our hands on them?"

"I'd like an answer to that question myself," Colum said. "Robert died trying to find those bones. He was a good man. He didn't deserve to lose his life over a centuries old corpse."

"He didn't lose his life in vain. I promise you that." Hunt leaned forward and lowered his voice. "Grendel was real. His longevity was no myth. Once we have his remains in our possession, we'll be able to analyze them and find out why he possessed such an extraordinarily long lifespan. That knowledge could upend the pharmaceuticals industry overnight, save millions of lives, and lead to drugs that will change the course of humanity."

"You think Grendel's bones are some magical fountain of youth," Decker said, the ramifications of Hunt's words dawning upon him. "You want to use them to extend human life."

"Not just extend," Hunt whispered. "A treatment derived from Grendel's remains could open the door to immortality…"

THIRTY-EIGHT

LATER THAT NIGHT Decker sat propped up on the bed in his cramped accommodations above the Claddagh's barroom, which was quiet now, the pub having closed thirty minutes since. In his lap was an iPad displaying a page about longevity research that he'd found on the Internet. It wasn't much help. Talk of extending human life by five, ten, or even twenty years was a far cry from the virtual immortality Hunt hoped to achieve with Grendel's remains. He wondered if the lofty goal was even possible. Grendel would surely be nothing but a pile of dusty old bones by now. Even if DNA could be successfully extracted, there was no guarantee that any genetic markers linked to extended lifespan could be isolated or used in any practical application. Indeed, most research pointed to genetic predispositions for disease being the biggest contributing factor to the number of years a person lived. He had read nothing in his albeit brief web-based sojourn into genetics that made a case for any specific places within a DNA molecule that could, by themselves, directly affect longevity in the population at large. That Grendel's remains contained some hitherto undiscovered answer to one of genetics Holy Grail's was, in Decker's opinion, far-fetched. Even so, he wondered how much CUSP knew that they were keeping to themselves. It seemed unlikely they would embark upon a quest such as this without some form of prior knowledge that rendered the time and costs worthwhile.

He was still pondering this when there was a soft knock at the door.

Decker put the iPad down and jumped off the bed. When he answered, Hunt was standing on the other side.

"You're still up. Good."

"What's going on?" Decker asked.

"Grab a coat and come with me," Hunt replied. "We're going on a little drive."

"We are?" Decker's gaze fell to the object Hunt was carrying in one hand. "Why do you have a crowbar?"

"To tear that padlock off the door leading to the caves." Hunt met Decker's gaze. "The landlord keeps a toolbox in the beer cellar. This seemed like the easiest way to achieve that goal."

"I thought we were staying away from the caves."

"We were. This afternoon," Hunt replied. "I wanted to assess our options before I settled upon a course of action. Breaking into the caves would appear to be the swiftest way to achieve our goals. It's that or we waste time going through official channels, blow our cover here, and risk drawing unwarranted attention to ourselves. Are you in?"

"Why not? Sergeant Byrne's attitude today rankled me. Besides, it's unlikely he'll know that we were there, especially if we cover our tracks well enough."

"My thoughts exactly."

"If you're going up to the caves, I'm coming too." A new voice interrupted their conversation. Hunt and Decker looked around to see Astrid standing in her bedroom door, a determined look upon her face.

"Absolutely not." Hunt shook his head. "I want this operation limited to as few people as possible."

"I'm coming with you, and that's all there is to it." The tone of Astrid's voice left little doubt regarding her intention to accompany them. "This is my dig. Anyway, you won't find Grendel's remains without me."

"Astrid has a point," Decker noted. "Maybe we should bring her along."

"Very well." Hunt sighed, then spoke again in a half whisper. "If you're both ready, let's go."

"What about the car keys," Decker asked. "Doesn't Colum have them?"

Hunt tapped his pocket. "I've already secured the car keys. Colum and Rory will stay here and provide cover for us, if necessary. I've already provided them with a plausible story that we returned to Dublin to deal with an urgent but unrelated matter regarding a dig elsewhere. Astrid's absence, should it be discovered, will play into that scenario very nicely."

"Hang on a moment," Decker said. He ducked back into his room and picked up the TV remote, clicking on the small TV that was affixed to the wall opposite the bed. He turned the sound up so that it would be audible outside of the room. "Might as well make it sound like I'm home."

"If you're ready." Hunt turned and strode down the corridor without waiting for the others. Decker grabbed his room key and a jacket, then stepped into the corridor, pulling the door closed behind him. That done, he and Astrid hurried after Hunt, who was already halfway down the stairs.

They slipped out of the pub's side door and across to the Land Rover. Decker and Astrid climbed into the back. Hunt took a tour around the vehicle, checking the tires to make sure there was no further damage. Satisfied that the vehicle was in good running order, he climbed into the driver's seat. Before starting the car, he snapped the headlight controls from automatic to the off position.

"No point in drawing more attention than unnecessary," he

said, reversing the darkened car from the parking space and turning onto Winslow Road.

He drove a few miles under the speed limit until they exited the village, and then sped up, snapping the headlights back on as he did so. Up ahead, swathed in darkness, was the monastery, and Grendel's bones.

THIRTY-NINE

HARRY REARDON WAS in his flat on the third floor of the Claddagh Arms preparing for bed when he heard a car door slam in the parking lot below. He dropped his toothbrush and rushed to the side window in time to see Adam Hunt climb into the Land Rover, start the engine, and drive off into the darkness without bothering to turn on his headlights. He went back to the bedroom and donned a bathrobe, then made his way down one floor to the guest accommodations.

All was quiet here, save for the sound of a TV coming from John Decker's room. Hunt, it appeared, had left on his own. Harry turned back to the stairs and was about to return to his flat when one of the bedroom doors opened and the Irishman, Colum, appeared wearing nothing but a pair of red boxer shorts.

"Can I help you, Harry?" Colum asked.

"It's all fine," Harry said. "I saw Adam Hunt depart in the Land Rover and wondered if there was a problem."

"Nope." Colum folded his arms. "Mr. Hunt had to return to Dublin to deal with an issue. He'll be back before dawn, I'm sure."

"Nothing serious, I hope." Harry didn't believe for one

second that Adam Hunt had departed for Dublin. For a start, he turned in the wrong direction when he left the parking lot. The more likely scenario was that he was heading to the monastery, just as Sergeant Byrne had predicted he would.

"Just a routine matter." Colum met the landlord's gaze. If he was lying, he showed no sign of it.

"Very well then," Harry said, then turned to retreat back upstairs. "I'll see you all at breakfast."

"You can count on that." Colum stepped back into the room and closed the door.

Harry made his way back upstairs, then picked up his cell phone and called Sergeant Byrne.

The policeman answered after one ring.

"I just thought you should know, Adam Hunt is on his way to the monastery," Harry said without waiting for the sergeant to speak.

"Is he now?" Sergeant Byrne sounded tired. Harry wondered if he'd woken him up. "Who else is with him?"

"He's the only one I saw leave. I went down and checked on the others, just to be sure."

"You did good, Harry." The sergeant sounded more awake now. Harry could hear him moving around, presumably preparing to leave and chase after Hunt. "Make sure the others stay where they are. I'll deal with them as soon as I've intercepted Adam Hunt."

"They can't go anywhere, they don't have a vehicle," Harry observed. "I'll keep a watch out, anyway."

"Good, good. Let me know if they make any moves," Byrne said, then hung up.

Harry put the phone back on his nightstand and sat on the bed. He didn't like Aiden Byrne. The local Garda was, in Harry's opinion, lazy. On top of that, he drank too much. The group from UNESCO who occupied the rooms below him were putting money in his pocket, and Harry felt bad spying on them, but he also understood the need to protect the village's dark secret. He would, as Sergeant Byrne had requested, keep an eye on the outsiders, albeit grudgingly. To do otherwise might lead to questions no one in Clareconnell was willing to answer.

FORTY

THE LAND ROVER drove through the dark lanes, its headlights lancing the night and illuminating the bushes and trees on each side of the narrow road. Hunt hadn't said a word since leaving Clareconnell behind, but now he spoke, addressing Astrid who sat next to Decker in the back.

"Have you got any idea where the bones are located?"

"I think so." Astrid looked out of the window, at the dark landscape whipping past. "Robert thought they would be fairly close to the cave opening. I disagreed. I thought the Danes would have buried him further in to minimize the chance of anyone disturbing his remains."

"Why were they even worried about that?" Decker asked. "He was dead. He couldn't hurt anyone."

"They thought the bones possessed magical powers." Astrid turned from the window. "Even in death, they were afraid of Grendel. That's why they took the trouble to transport him so far from their homeland, risking a dangerous sea journey and then a march through a hostile land. Even the locals feared him. Decades after his interment, they built the monastery over the labyrinth as a precaution. The monks viewed the caves as a godless place, an entrance to hell itself."

"I want to be in and out of the caves as quickly as possible," Hunt said. "Will you know the bones when you see them?"

"Yes." Astrid nodded. "I've done extensive research. The grave will be well marked."

"There's something we're all forgetting here," Decker said. "We still don't know what dragged Robert off."

"An excellent question," Hunt replied. "I fear there is more in those caves than dust and bones. I would suggest we exercise supreme caution while we are down there. I also posit that whatever dragged Robert off is the reason that Sergeant Byrne is so keen to keep us away."

"Perhaps we should have brought weapons with us." Decker was beginning to think that this midnight expedition was too risky.

"An excellent suggestion." Hunt glanced into the back, then quickly returned his eyes to the road. "I would love nothing more than to have a couple of guns at hand. Unfortunately, that is not an option. We'll have to make do with caution, and the crowbar I found."

"It would have taken something mighty big to drag off a full-size man," Decker said. "I'm not sure the crowbar will be enough if we run across whatever took him."

"We were working up at that monastery for weeks and never came across anything bigger than a rabbit," Astrid said. "I don't know what happened to Robert, but I find it hard to believe he was dragged off by anything in those caves. It's more likely that a human took him, although why they would bother is beyond me."

"That cave system could run for miles, and we have no idea if there are any other entrances," Hunt said. The monastery had appeared now, looming out of the darkness across the fields. Hunt slowed and turned the car onto the dirt track leading to the ruins. "Astrid may be correct. It's always possible that someone from the village took Robert's body. However, I think we should keep an open mind, and our wits about us. This village is not all it seems, and I fear that the missing body is just one piece in a larger puzzle."

"Maybe we should have brought Colum with us after all," Decker said. "If we run into anything unexpected in those caves it would be nice to have some extra muscle around."

"I'm sure we can handle this ourselves." Hunt brought the Land Rover to a halt under the shadow of the monastery walls. They climbed out and made their way toward the ruins, flashlights in hand. Above them, clouds scudded across the sky, covering the moon at intervals, which only deepened the darkness.

"It's creepy up here," Astrid said, pushing herself close to Decker. "I wish we could do this in daylight."

"I doubt we'd get away with it during the day," Hunt said. "Besides, it's just as dark in the caves at all times of day and night."

They picked their way through the remains of what used to be the monastery's nave, and onward into the south transept where the hole leading to the crypt yawned.

Decker descended first, keeping his flashlight aimed downward onto the treacherous steps to make sure that he didn't slip and fall. Next came Astrid, picking her way down at a painfully slow pace. When Hunt joined them, the trio set off through the outer room toward the door carved with demons.

But something was not right.

The carved door, padlocked and secure only hours before, was now standing wide open.

FORTY-ONE

BARRY CLAMAGH WAS TUCKED up in bed when he heard the first alarmed squawks coming from the direction of his chicken barns. He rose, grumbling, and went to the window. Chickens attracted foxes, and there was no shortage of the vermin sniffing around the farm on any given day. He wondered if one had somehow gotten inside a barn to terrorize the startled birds within.

He pulled the curtain aside and peered through the darkness toward the farmyard. Fifty feet away stood the closest of the chicken barns. In the space between it and the house Barry saw a flock of small pale forms milling around in panic. Chickens. He also saw the reason they were loose. The barn doors stood wide open. This nixed the idea that a fox had gained entry. Foxes didn't open doors.

He cursed, pulling on a pair of jeans and a denim shirt.

"What's going on?" Lucy mumbled from the bed, still half asleep.

"I don't know yet. The chickens got loose." Barry was at the bedroom door now. He glanced back toward the bed, where his wife, Lucy, had propped herself up on her elbows. "I won't be long. Go back to sleep."

"Be careful." Lucy yawned and snuggled back down under the covers. She was used to her husband stepping out at all hours of day and night to tend to one issue or another on the farm. "I don't want to have to drive you to Kilkenny because you got bitten by a fox."

"Don't be daft, woman. Why would I get bitten by anything?" He turned and pulled the door closed behind him, then raced downstairs to the gun cabinet in his study. Moments later, armed with a shotgun, he was at the back door.

He paused, wondering if he should call Sergeant Byrne. Foxes might not be able to unlatch the door, but humans could. Barry was not well liked in the village thanks to his decision to align himself with the industrialized poultry industry at the expense of the other farmers hereabouts. This didn't bother him, but sabotage did. One of the other farmers, it seemed, had decided to level the playing field. He felt the anger bubble up inside of him. The most likely candidate was Sean O'Mara. The man had made his feelings clear the previous day, walking off the job and leaving it half done. Barry had been forced to put the last stair treads on himself. This fact only reinforced the belief that he'd been right in underpaying. Half a job deserved half a paycheck. Well, Barry didn't need a local Garda to take care of a snake like Sean O'Mara.

He pulled the door open, gun at the ready, and started across the farmyard. Chickens squabbled and clucked as he passed by, scrabbling to get out of the way. At the barn door he stopped and checked the gun to make certain it was loaded, then raised it.

"If there's anyone in there, I'm giving you fair warning, I'm armed." Barry shouted through the doorway into the cavernous space beyond. He waited to see if there was a reply. His only answer was the terrified clucking of chickens.

"I'm coming in," Barry said, hoping that his warning would give pause to anyone hiding in the darkness.

He stepped across the threshold, beyond the opened doors,

then reached to his left and clicked on the lights. The barn lit up in dim yellow illumination that struggled to reach the furthest corners of the massive space.

All around him milled chickens, some, seeing their opportunity, staggering toward the open doors and freedom on spindly legs barely able to support their genetically modified obese bodies. Others, too weak to move, stayed where they were and squawked in wide-eyed terror.

Barry ignored the chickens and peered around the barn, looking for the source of their consternation. At first, he didn't see anything, but then his eyes settled upon the shape squatting down at the back near the wall.

He took a step forward.

"Who are you?" Barry asked, the gun still raised, his finger light on the trigger. "Speak up."

The crouched figure did not speak up. It lifted its head to look at him, and in that moment, Barry saw the dead chicken clutched in its hands, and the blood that dripped from its chin. Worse than that was the grotesque face that peered back at him, more beast the man.

"Holy Shite." The gun trembled in Barry's hands. "What in God's name are you?"

The creature reared up, dropping the half-eaten chicken and staring at him.

Barry recoiled. Instead of an animal, he found himself looking into a pair of sparkling blue eyes that met his gaze with cool intelligence.

"Stay right where you are," Barry said, unable to hide the fear in his voice. The more he looked at the creature, the more human it became. It even had tufts of silky blonde hair growing from its leathery, pockmarked scalp.

The beast did not stay where it was. It started toward him with grim determination.

"I'm warning you, I'll shoot," Barry said, but even as he spoke the words, he felt his bravado slipping away. Try as he might, he couldn't will his finger to pull the trigger. It was one thing to shoot a fox, but quite another to shoot something that looked so human. Instead, he backed up toward the open doors, ignoring the chickens that screeched and scrabbled to move out of his way.

The beast kept on coming. Faster now.

Barry found the will to fire the gun. The boom was deafening; the sound echoing around the barn, but instead of dropping the beast, Barry's shot went wide. He fired again, discharging the other cartridge. If he scored a hit, the creature showed no sign of it. Instead, it glared at him and let out a growl of anger.

The last of Barry's nerves abandoned him. He dropped the gun and turned, fleeing in blind panic toward the doors. He leapt over chickens, weaved through them, until he reached the threshold. Then, just as he thought he was going to escape, the monster caught up with him. It grabbed the back of his shirt, around the collar, and yanked him backwards.

Barry let out a startled screech, legs flailing and kicking up dirt, as he was dragged back into the barn. He squirmed and punched, frantic to get free, but to no avail. Then, as the beast started in on him, chewing and tearing, Barry screamed, his agonized cries merging with the frightened squawks of countless chickens…

FORTY-TWO

"WHY IS THE DOOR OPEN?" Astrid asked, concern in her voice. "Do you think the sergeant came back and unlocked it again?"

"Unlikely." Decker closed the gap and examined the door. "The padlock is still attached. This door has been forced open."

"And from the inside, it would appear," Hunt said. He placed the crowbar on the ground inside the tunnel and ran his fingers along the doorframe, and the splintered wood where the screws had held the hasp in place. "I would hazard a guess that whatever took Robert objected to being locked in."

"At least we know the caves are safe now," Decker observed, noticing the large iron bolt that was attached to the door. "Sergeant Byrne should have pulled this bolt across rather than bothering to secure the door with a padlock."

"A bolt only keeps whatever is inside from escaping," Hunt replied. "It doesn't stop people on the outside from entering. A padlock will achieve both things at once."

"Except that it didn't keep anything from escaping. Whatever was on the other side of this door merely barged through using brute strength."

"Quite." Hunt stepped back into the crypt. "This changes nothing. We should proceed and see what we can find."

But before they could move, a voice drifted down from above. It was Sergeant Byrne.

"Mr. Hunt. I know you're down there. I would appreciate it if you would step back up here so we can have a little talk."

Decker and Hunt exchanged a glance. How Sergeant Byrne had known they were at the monastery, Decker had no idea. The most likely explanation was that Harry heard the Land Rover leave and called him.

"I'm waiting, Mr. Hunt. I would prefer not to come down there, but I will."

Decker took Astrid's arm and steered her into the darkness of the tunnel. It appeared that Sergeant Byrne believed that Hunt was on his own.

"I'll have to go up," Hunt whispered. "He's not going to let this lie, and I don't want him to discover the two of you."

"He threatened to arrest anyone he caught down here," Decker said.

"That's a risk I must take." Hunt motioned for them to stay where they were and stepped toward the outer room. When he reached the stone staircase, he glanced back. Then he started up toward the surface.

Decker stepped into the tunnel next to Astrid and clicked off his flashlight. The darkness was absolute and immediate. Up above he could hear faint voices, but he could not make out the words. Then, after a few minutes, there was silence. To be safe, he waited another couple of minutes in the tunnel before he clicked the flashlight back on and motioned to Astrid to follow him back to the steps. They ascended to the surface. As expected, Sergeant Byrne had departed, along with Adam Hunt, who had been placed under arrest, no doubt. They were alone.

FORTY-THREE

LUCY CLAMAGH SETTLED back into bed and closed her eyes, drifting back off to sleep as Barry hurried downstairs to deal with the chicken situation. It wasn't unusual for her husband to step outside at an ungodly hour to deal with some emergency or other. That was just life on the farm. She heard him tromping through the house below. Then came the dull thud as he closed the back door.

The house became silent once more.

The faint cluck of chickens filtered up from the farmyard but soon even that faded as Lucy sank back into a light and dreamless sleep.

How long she dozed, Lucy had no idea, but she was soon jolted awake by the crack of a gun going off. Moments later there was another sharp report. Barry must have found the fox. She lay in bed and listened for his return.

Minutes ticked by.

The chickens, momentarily shocked into silence by the sudden gunshots, resumed their squawking.

Lucy sat up. Barry should have been back by now. A tingle of foreboding prickled up her spine. She swung her legs off the bed and stood up, then went to the window and peered out. The farmyard was dark and empty, only a single lamp secured to a pole halfway between the farmhouse and the row of chicken Barns gave any illumination. It was woefully inadequate but provided enough light to confirm that Barry was not on his way back. The doors of the closest barn stood open, which meant that her husband was still inside. Lucy stood there for a while, hoping that Barry would reappear. When it became evident that he was not going to, she padded to her wardrobe and removed the dressing gown from a wire hanger. After slipping it on and tying the belt she hurried downstairs and through the house to the back door. She stepped out into the night and made her way across the farmyard, ignoring the chickens. They were fat and slow. They would be easy to catch and put back in the barn after she'd found Barry.

When she reached the barn door, Lucy paused.

"Barry?" She hissed her husband's name in a low voice, expecting him to reply. Only the gabble of excited poultry answered her. "Barry, for the love of God, are you in there?"

Still no response.

Lucy took a step forward, wavered, and then stepped back, away from the door. She didn't know why, but she was over-come by a sudden conviction that danger lurked inside the barn. She pulled her dressing gown tight around her thin frame and waited another minute, hoping that Barry would appear and save her the trouble of venturing inside. She almost turned and fled back to the safety of the farmhouse, but that would do no good if Barry was still in here somewhere.

"Get a grip, Lucy Clamagh," she scolded herself. "It's just a chicken barn."

The self-admonishment did little to ease her fears, but she returned to the barn door anyway. Taking a deep breath, she ventured within.

The entire floor was packed with chickens that watched her with beady black eyes as she picked her way to the center of the barn. She looked around yet saw no sign of her husband.

"Barry, are you in here?" She spoke the words in a hoarse whisper, hoping her husband would hear them, but at the same time fearful. Even though she couldn't see a threat, the primitive side of her brain, the amygdala, was screaming danger.

Lucy Clamagh decided that she didn't want to be there anymore. Besides, for all she knew, Barry was in one of the other barns. She turned to retreat back toward the doors, but then her eyes settled on a strange sight at the front of the barn to the left of the entrance. A figure squatting low, head hunched down.

"Barry?" Lucy closed the gap between them. "Is that you? What are you doing?"

The figure did not respond.

She drew closer, a shiver of fear crawling up her spine, because now she saw that it wasn't one figure. It was two. The first sitting astride the other with its head bent low. A sucking, slurping sound reached her ears, which only stopped when the figure looked up. A guttural cough escaped its lips, both human and animalistic at the same time. It rose to its feet, giving her a clear view of the prone body laying beneath. Lucy let out a gasp, her hands flying to her mouth in horror. Sprawled motionless on the ground was Barry, his neck covered by what looked like a red bandana. Only it wasn't a bandana, she realized. It was blood that spurted from a wide swath of ripped flesh and trickled down to soak the dirt floor.

Lucy stumbled backward.

The chickens flapped and bustled to get out of her way, but her feet got tied up and she fell. Her head smacked into the ground, and for a moment her vision faded to black. She fought through the pain and tried to sit up, even as the ghastly figure, which she now saw was a hideous beast, naked, with bulging muscles and skin like parchment, advanced upon her.

She scooted backward, a shriek of terror forcing its way up. Then, just as the scream found its way to her lips, the beast leaped forward...

FORTY-FOUR

DECKER and Astrid stood in the nave of the ruined monastery, their flashlights doing little to penetrate the darkness.

"What are we going to do now?" Astrid asked.

"I don't know," Decker answered. They were miles from the village and even though he could see the Land Rover still parked where they had left it outside of the monastery's ruined walls, they had no keys. Those were in Adam Hunt's pocket. Decker cursed his stupidity for not reminding Hunt to give him the keys while they were down in the caverns before Sergeant Byrne arrested him. "I think our only option is to walk back to Clareconnell."

"That will take hours, and its pitch black out here. We'll be lucky if we don't fall into a ditch and break our legs. I think we should go back into the caves and retrieve Grendel's bones. Sergeant Byrne taking Adam away doesn't change anything. We still have a job to do and might not get another chance to do it."

"Too risky." Decker shook his head. "If the sergeant realizes we're missing, he'll come back to search for us. Even if he doesn't discover that we're up here, he may very well return to secure that door again and then we'd be trapped underground."

"I suppose you're right," Astrid said, clearly disappointed.

"I don't like it any more than you," Decker replied. He placed a hand on her shoulder. "Come on, it's a long walk back to the village. We might as well get started."

"Or you could call Colum to come pick us up."

"With what?" Decker asked. "The CUSP field office had your car collected by the rental company. I guess they figured that since it was in your colleague's name, and we had the Land Rover, there was no need for it."

"We should at least tell them what's happening."

"You're right," Decker said. "They need to know that Sergeant Byrne is on the warpath. We might as well start to walk back to the village. I'll make the call as we go."

Astrid nodded. They left the nave behind and followed the trail through fields toward the road. Decker took out his phone and placed a call to Colum, filling him in on the turn of events. The Irishman fired off a couple of annoyed expletives that ended with the suggestion that he go down to the Garda station, kick the door in, and liberate Hunt by force. None of this was helpful and Decker told the ex-ranger as much. When he and Astrid arrived back at the village, they would formulate a plan to spring their leader out of jail through more diplomatic means. Colum grudgingly agreed, and Decker hung up, fairly sure that the Irishman would not do anything rash in the meantime.

"What do you think broke out of the caves?" Astrid asked as they rejoined the main road in the direction of Clareconnell.

"That's a very good question," Decker answered. "Whatever, or whoever it is must possess exceptional strength to bust open the door like that."

"And now it's on the loose." Astrid looked around at the dark fields that fell away on each side of the road. "What if we run into it?"

"I hadn't considered that." Decker had been so consumed with the sergeant showing up at the monastery, and them being stranded so far from the village in the middle of the night, that he hadn't given any thought to the possibility that whatever escaped the caves was close by. His mind wandered back to the conversation Sergeant Byrne had engaged in the previous day with the young woman from the village. Her husband was missing. This felt like a big coincidence, and Decker wasn't sure he believed in coincidence. It was prudent, he decided, to assume that whatever had left the caves was dangerous. Even so, he didn't want to worry Astrid unnecessarily, so he did his best to reassure her. "I'm sure whatever got out of those caves is miles away by now."

"If you think so." Astrid didn't look particularly reassured.

"I do," Decker said, but he couldn't help looking out over the dark fields anyway, just to make sure…

FORTY-FIVE

SERGEANT BYRNE LED HUNT into the Garda station and to the pair of cells in the converted cottage's smaller room. He pushed Hunt into the closer of the two and slammed the door. Hunt heard the locks engage, and then a panel set high in the door slid back. Byrne peered in at him.

"I'm going to round up your friends, and then we're going to have that chat."

"I'm not sure this arrest is legal," Hunt said, glaring at the policeman.

"Go ahead and call your solicitor." Byrne chuckled and drew the panel back across the observation window. This was followed, a few seconds later, by the sound of the Garda station door closing.

Hunt swore. The sergeant knew damned well that he couldn't place a call to a lawyer—or solicitor as they were known in Ireland—because Byrne had confiscated his cell phone moments after placing him under arrest. The charge—trespassing—was bogus, and the policeman knew it. The monastery was not private property and CUSP had all the permits required to conduct an excavation there. There was even less rationale for taking those members of the group who were still at the hotel into custody. They had not even violated Sergeant Byrne's dubiously enforceable order to stay away from the dig site.

Hunt paced back and forth in the cell for a while, his fists clenching and unclenching in silent rage. Then, once the anger had given way to grudging acceptance, he took a seat on a concrete ledge covered by a thin mattress. He leaned back against the cell wall and closed his eyes, centering his emotions. He cleared his mind and analyzed the situation, weighing his options, which appeared to be limited. At least in the short term.

He was still pondering this when Sergeant Byrne returned and unlocked the door. "He's in here."

Colum and Rory peered into the cell.

"Hey, boss," Colum said. "We'll get you out of here in a jiffy."

"Actually, I'm going to need you to join your boss in the cell," Byrne said.

"What? Why?" Colum looked confused.

"Just do as I say." Byrne ushered Colum and Rory inside, then quickly backtracked, slamming the door closed and locking it.

Colum whirled around. "What the hell?"

The panel in the door slid open. "The pair of you are under arrest too, now pipe down."

"Under arrest? What for?" Colum exclaimed. He turned to Hunt. "He told us that if we accompanied him here and answered his questions, he'd release you."

"I can't believe you fell for that." Hunt sat back down on the mattress ledge.

Rory took a seat next to him. He glanced up at Colum. "It looks like we were played."

"This is bullshit." Colum turned back toward the door and pounded a fist against it. "You have no right to detain us like this."

"I have every right." Byrne glared through the opening. "Now keep quiet in there."

"If you wanted me quiet you shouldn't have arrested me."

Colum kicked the door. "I'm warning you, open that door and let me out right now."

"Or what?"

"Or I'll kick the feckin thing down and then start in on you."

"That sounds like you're threatening a Garda officer." Byrne smiled. "That's an offense right there."

"Give me half a chance and I'll commit a few more offenses."

"That's enough." Hunt motioned for Colum to join them on the bench. "This isn't getting us anywhere."

Colum glared through the viewing window at Byrne then turned and stomped over to the bench.

"That's better." Byrne turned his attention to Hunt. "Now, why don't you tell me where the last two members of your group are."

"I don't know where they are." Hunt shrugged.

"You're lying," Byrne said, a fleck of annoyance in his voice. "I thought you were alone up at the monastery. It appears I was wrong. I assume they're up there right now attempting to break into the caves."

"They don't need to break into the caves." Hunt stood and moved close to the door, his face inches from the small rectangular viewing window. "Something had already broken out. The door was wide open when we got there."

"What do you mean?" Now Sergeant Byrne's voice quivered with fear rather than annoyance.

"The door was smashed open from inside. Your padlock didn't do much to contain whatever was down there." Hunt kept his voice low and even. "I must conclude that you've known something was in the caves all along. That would explain why you've been so reticent to accompany us underground. It also explains why Robert's body went missing."

"I thought the door would hold," Sergeant Byrne said, caught off guard. Then he pulled himself together. "If your friends are up there, if they went into those caves, you'd better hope it's not still in there with them."

"Why?" Hunt asked, his anger returning. "What exactly *is* in those caves?"

But Sergeant Byrne didn't answer. Instead he drew the metal panel back over the viewing window and latched it. Hunt heard him move off into the main office. A few minutes later the front door banged shut. It appeared that the sergeant had left again, presumably to go in search of Astrid and Decker...

FORTY-SIX

DECKER AND ASTRID spent the next few miles walking in silence. The thought that they were not alone in the Irish countryside had left Decker feeling uneasy, and he sensed that Astrid felt the same. She moved closer to him as they walked, her shoulder brushing his.

"Are you doing okay?" Decker asked, after a while.

"Yes." Astrid smiled. "I feel safe with you around."

"Good." He noticed that she was shivering, despite the light sweater she wore. The temperature had been dropping gradually ever since they left the monastery, and now a stiff wind blew over the fields, adding to their discomfort. He'd put a jacket on before they left the pub, knowing the caves would be cold, and now he took it off and draped it over her shoulders, then put his arm around her. When she glanced at him, he shrugged. "You were shivering."

"That's so sweet." She moved closer still, her own arm sliding around his waist. "I'll be glad when we get back to the village. I don't like it out here. I can't stop thinking about that door, the way it was broken open."

"I won't let any harm come to you," Decker said. "I promise."

"I don't know why, but I believe you," Astrid said. "You're very self-assured for someone on their first assignment."

"This might be my first job with CUSP, but I've had my share of close calls," Decker said.

"Like what?" Astrid asked. "If you don't mind me asking?"

"Not at all." Decker told her about his time as a cop in New York, and his move back to Wolf Haven. When he spoke of the killings there, he omitted the fact that Annie Doucet had turned herself into the Loup-garou, leaving Astrid to assume that a crazed animal had committed the attacks. When he told her about his tangle in the Central Florida woodlands, she raised an eyebrow.

"You don't seem to have much luck with wildlife," she said. "I'm beginning to think it might not be safe to walk with you, after all. I don't want anything to eat me."

Decker laughed, despite his dour mood. "If a wild animal attacks us, I'll let it chew on me while you make your escape. How about that."

"Sounds like a fine plan," Astrid laughed now. "I only hope there's enough meat on your bones to give it a good meal, otherwise it will come after me anyway."

"I'll do my best to sate it," Decker replied. "But enough about me. It's your turn. Talk."

"What would you like to know?"

"Well, for a start, why are you so obsessed with Grendel, and how did you end up working for Hunt?"

"I don't know why Grendel became more important to me than anything else," Astrid replied. "I've wanted to find him for as long as I can remember. I always knew that he wasn't a myth, some fictional character in an old poem. I became an archaeologist so that I could track him. I've traveled through much of Scandinavia, excavated burial mounds, Viking settlements. Eventually I came to believe that the Danes had taken him somewhere else. Somewhere far away from his homeland. When Adam Hunt and CUSP came to me looking for an expert and showed me the manuscript they'd found, I knew my hunch was right."

"So here you are."

"Yes, here I am." Astrid stopped and looked around. "How much further do you think it is back to the village? We must have been walking for an hour. My feet hurt."

"I'd say we're about halfway back," Decker said. He had Maps on his phone, and it occurred to him that it would tell them how far they had left to walk. He reached into his pocket to take the phone out, but then up ahead, he saw a faint glimmer of headlights coming toward them.

"A car," Astrid said. "Maybe they can give us a ride back to the village."

"They're heading in the wrong direction," Decker replied. There was nothing on this road but the ruined monastery, and only one reason why a car would be traveling there. He took Astrid and pushed her to the side of the road. "We should get out of sight."

"Why?" Astrid looked confused. "That car might be able to help us."

"I don't think so." Decker steered her to the side of the road and through a row of thick bushes that snagged their clothes. They emerged into a field and crouched down low.

They'd barely ducked out of sight when the car passed by, moving fast.

Decker caught a glimpse of the word Garda written in blue lettering below a fluorescent yellow stripe that ran the length of the vehicle.

Sergeant Byrne.

He was, no doubt, heading back up to the monastery to search for them. That was not good. It meant that he'd been to the Claddagh and knew that they were not there.

"That was close," Astrid said, as the police car receded into the distance.

"Too close." Decker watched the taillights disappear as the

ANTHONY M. STRONG

vehicle crested a rise and then went down the other side. He pushed the bushes aside for Astrid to step back onto the road and they set off once more toward the village.

FORTY-SEVEN

SERGEANT BYRNE STEPPED AWAY from the cells and returned to his office. He was mad. He should have anticipated that Adam Hunt would not be at the monastery alone, regardless of what Harry down at the Claddagh said. Now there were outsiders running around unaccounted for. Worse, if Hunt was correct, the beast from the caves was on the loose for a third night despite the sergeant's attempts to contain it. This was an unmitigated disaster. There had already been at least two fatal attacks, for Craig Hennessy and Father Cleary were surely dead.

Byrne groaned.

Why couldn't the beast have just taken the corpse of Tom Walsh and been satisfied, as it had in the past. He felt his frustration mounting all over again. If only those damned archaeologists had stayed away from the monastery none of this would be happening. Any blood would be on their hands, not his. He only hoped that the beast would come across a cow or a sheep to satisfy its appetite before it got as far as the village. Not that he held out much hope that it would. Grendel liked human flesh. He debated whether he should round up some of the other villagers, Harry Reardon and Sean O'Mara sprung to mind, and try to find the monster before it took another life. Except that would mean alerting the residents of Clareconnell to the danger in their midst, setting off a panic. It would also mean being exposed as a failure. What scared him the most though, was the thought of actually coming face-to-face with the beast. If in times of crisis great men were born, then by extension, cowardly men were exposed. It was better, Byrne thought, to keep quiet and hope for the best.

There was one upside to the creature having escaped its confinement. The caves would be safe. He could go up there and look for the two members of Adam Hunt's group who were still missing. The more he thought about it, the more it felt like the correct course of action. Once he'd gathered up the last of the outsiders and eliminated them from the equation, the beast could be easily contained by simply waiting until daylight, which Grendel abhorred. The creature's aversion to light was well known among the villagers. Many years ago, before Sergeant Byrne had taken over as Clareconnell's lone policeman, the pallbearers responsible for delivering dead bodies to the beast had returned to the offering chamber too soon. Grendel was still there, sniffing around the corpse. But when they turned the chamber's lights on, he screeched in pain and retreated, allowing them to close the inner door. After so much time living in the darkness of the caves, Grendel had become so sensitive to light that it caused him pain. Once the sun was up, he would retreat to his cavernous lair. At that point it would be a simple task to go under the monastery and re-secure the door. This time Sergeant Byrne would not make the mistake of using a flimsy padlock. A bunch of two by fours and the longest screws he could find should do the trick. With the beast back in its lair, the village would return to normal. Even better, Sergeant Byrne could take credit for resolving the situation without facing the creature.

It was the perfect plan.

His course of action decided, Sergeant Byrne scooped up the Garda cruiser's keys and headed for the door. Once outside, he hurried to the police car, hopped in, and set off in the direction of the monastery.

After leaving the village behind, Sergeant Byrne pushed the car ten miles past the speed limit, and faster than he would normally have dared in the narrow lanes surrounding the village. It was after 2 AM and everyone would be tucked up in bed. Not only that, the road to the monastery dead ended a mile past the ruins at an old farm long since out of business thanks to the encroachment of corporate agriculture. Now the land lay empty and up for sale.

He had the road to himself.

Byrne peered through the windshield and out into the darkness. Soon he came across the turnoff leading to the ruins and slowed, easing the car up the bumpy dirt trail and coming to a halt next to Adam Hunt's Land Rover.

He smiled.

The Land Rover's keys were on his desk back at the Garda station, along with Hunt's cell phone. He had confiscated both items as soon as he'd placed the annoying American under arrest. Astrid and Decker were surely still here. They had no way to get back to town unless they walked, and there was no sign of them out on the road.

Byrne climbed out of the car and grabbed his flashlight from the back seat, then made his way past the crumbling walls to the steps that wound into the crypt.

He peered into the hole, his stomach clenching in knots now that he was actually here. The beast was not down there, he was sure. It hadn't gone to the trouble of escaping only to linger within its prison. He glanced at his watch. There were still four hours until dawn, plenty of time to apprehend the last two members of Hunt's group and leave the caves before Grendel returned.

Sergeant Byrne took a tentative step onto the stone staircase. He shined the flashlight ahead of him and descended. When he reached the bottom he looked around, but there was no sign of his quarry. That did not surprise him. Their interest was centered around the caves. He had no idea why, and he didn't care. Perhaps they were still searching for the dead archaeologist's body, in the hope that they could retrieve him. If that were the case, they would be sorely disappointed. Byrne knew exactly what had happened to that body even if he didn't know where it was.

The sergeant moved off again, leaving the outer room behind and approaching the demon carved door. Here he stopped, examining the damage to his padlock and hasp, and then peered into the darkness beyond. He pointed the flashlight through the opening but saw no one.

"Is there anyone in there?" He shouted, his words echoing and bouncing off the cave walls. When he received no response, Byrne stepped beyond the door, into the caves.

It was then that he heard a noise coming from the crypt behind him.

Someone was descending the stairs, making no attempt to conceal their movement.

Byrne turned around and peered back into the crypt. He was about to raise the flashlight, then he thought better of it and instead clicked it off.

The darkness rushed in around him, absolute.

He could see nothing now, save for a shaft of weak moonlight filtering down through the hole in the ground where the staircase wound into the crypt. But it was what descended the stairs that raised the hairs on the sergeant's neck.

Grendel. And slung over his shoulders, one on each side, a pair of limp bodies.

Sergeant Byrne recoiled in horror.

The beast had returned sooner than expected, and it had brought two fresh victims. He wondered who they were, but then pushed the thought aside. Another moment and he would be discovered. He felt a stab of panic. Escaping back up the stone steps was not an option. The beast was positioned between himself and the surface.

He was trapped.

Left with no other place to go, Sergeant Byrne turned and stumbled blindly into the stygian labyrinth.

FORTY-EIGHT

IT WAS past three in the morning when Astrid and Decker arrived back at the Claddagh Arms. They let themselves in via the side entrance and hurried through the bar and up the stairs to their accommodations. Decker went straight to Colum's room and knocked. When he didn't get an answer, he moved on to Rory's room with the same result.

"Do you think the sergeant arrested them?" Astrid lingered in the corridor behind Decker, a worried expression on her face.

"Either that, or they're both exceptionally heavy sleepers." Decker stepped away from the door. If the local Garda had taken Rory and Colum into custody, then he would come right back to the Claddagh as soon as he discovered that they were not at the monastery. Their arrest was all but guaranteed, and even if the sergeant couldn't formally press charges, he could certainly hold them in the cells for a day or two. This was soon confirmed by the appearance of Harry, the landlord, from his flat on the third floor.

"If you're looking for those friends of yours, don't bother. Byrne already came and dragged them off. He told me to call him right away if the pair of you showed up."

"Which I'm assuming you have already done," Decker said, turning toward the landlord.

Harry nodded. "I did. Or rather I tried. All I got was his voicemail. I left a message but who knows when he'll get it. He's probably tucked up in bed by now."

"He was on his way to the monastery an hour ago," Astrid said. "He passed us on the road."

"Makes sense. He was pretty mad that you disobeyed his order to stay away from the ruins," Harry replied. "You're in luck though. The reception up there is sketchy at best. That buys you a little time."

"It doesn't do us much good," Decker noted. "There's nowhere we can go that he wouldn't find us. We don't even have any transportation."

"That's a fine pickle you're in," Harry said. "I can't say I have any suggestions for you, other than getting some sleep while you can. The sergeant's cells aren't known for their comfort. Now if it's all the same with you, I'm back off to bed myself."

Decker nodded. "Thanks, Harry. It was good of you to warn us of the sergeant's intentions."

"Don't mention it." Harry started back up the stairs toward the third floor. "Having my guests end up in jail isn't good for business. I want to make sure you pay the bill when you check out, that's all."

Decker watched Harry depart and then turned to Astrid. "We need to call CUSP and get that sergeant reigned in."

"Are you sure that's wise?" Astrid asked. "Adam wanted to keep a low profile around here."

"I don't see what choice we have," Decker replied. "If we don't, we'll end up under arrest too. This is the only way if we want to ever step foot in those caves again."

"If you're sure."

"I am." Decker took out the phone Adam Hunt had given him when they arrived in Ireland. He opened the contacts but there was no number there for the shadowy organization. Other than Nancy, who appeared on the call log, the phone was a blank slate. He slipped it back into his pocket. "No luck. I'll have Harry let me into Hunt's room. He must have a way of contacting the field office."

"Wait." Astrid put hand out and stopped Decker as he was moving toward the stairs in the direction of the third floor. "What about the email address I've been using to send progress reports on the dig?"

"That should work," Decker said.

"Perfect. Give me a few minutes to freshen up and I'll bring my laptop over to your room and we'll send a message."

Decker nodded. "Okay, but don't take too long. I want this taken care of before the sergeant returns from the monastery."

"I know." Astrid moved off toward her room and slipped inside, closing the door softly behind her.

Decker watched her leave and then entered his own room. He sat down on the end of the bed and took his shoes off, grateful to give his aching feet room to breathe. He sighed. Hunt's plan to break into the caves had ended in disaster. If they couldn't get a message through to CUSP, Decker and Astrid would end up in the cells alongside the rest of the group, and Grendel's bones would remain where they were. At least in the short term. Although now that he thought about it, Decker wondered if Grendel's remains were even in the caves. Something had broken through that door. Something big and powerful. Was it possible that Hunt knew what was down there, or at least suspected it? Was that why Decker had been brought along on this trip? He was, after all, recruited to CUSP based on his run-ins with what could only be described as monsters. He stood and went to the window, gazing out over the dark landscape. Was there a creature out there right now, running free? He was still pondering this when there was a light knock at the door.

When he answered, Astrid was standing in the hallway wearing a flannel dressing gown that was tied around her waist. She held a bottle of wine and two glasses in her hands.

"Can I come in?"

Decker eyed the wine. "Where's the laptop? We have to send that email."

"I took care of it as soon as I got into my room," she said. "I was afraid that Sergeant Byrne would come back and thought it was better to send right away, just in case."

"I thought we were going to send it together," Decker said, surprised.

"I'm sorry." Astrid looked distressed. Her bottom lip trembled. "I thought I was helping. Did I do something wrong?"

"No." Decker shook his head. "It's fine. As long as the message was sent." He nodded toward the bottle and glasses. "What's that for?"

"A nightcap. I can't imagine I'm going to be able to get any sleep until this is settled, so I thought we could have a drink." Astrid looked at Decker with wide eyes. "Are you going to make me stand in the hallway all night?"

"Come on in." Decker stepped aside to let her into the room.

"You're a gentleman." Astrid stepped inside and placed the wine glasses on the nightstand next to Decker's bed, then unscrewed the wine bottle's cap and poured two large glasses. She held one out to Decker.

He took the glass. "You just happened to have a bottle of wine in your room?"

"Why not? I like wine." Astrid untied the bathrobe's belt and shrugged the garment off, letting it fall to the floor. Underneath, she was clad only in a thin satin night dress that ended at her thighs. The material clung to her body, accentuating her curves. "That's better."

"Don't you think that's a little revealing?" Decker asked.

"I just want to be comfortable." Astrid sat down on the bed and motioned for Decker to join her. "You're not embarrassed, are you?"

"No. I'm just not sure this is entirely appropriate."

"Don't be so silly." Astrid stood back up and went to Decker.

She reached out and ran a finger down his cheek, her body close to his. "It's nothing."

"Astrid, I'm in a relationship." Decker couldn't deny that he was tempted. She was beautiful, and Nancy's refusal of his marriage proposal had left him confused and hurt. He wondered how much longer he would be in a relationship. That didn't change things right now though.

"So?" Astrid was unfazed. She took Decker's hand, led him to the bed and sat, pulling him down alongside her. She turned and kissed him, her lips finding his, brushing them.

The kiss was soft and sweet and full of promise. It took all of Decker's will power to pull back instead of wrapping his arms around her and slipping the nightgown's thin straps from her shoulders. "I can't. I'm sorry."

She looked hurt, her blue eyes wide and vulnerable. "That's too bad John, I thought we had a special connection. But at least share a glass of wine with me."

"Just one glass." Decker sipped his wine. It wasn't, he noted, a particularly good bottle, leaving a slightly sour aftertaste on his pallet.

Astrid drank her own wine, watching him. When the glass was empty, she reached for the bottle, to top them up.

"I believe I've had enough." Decker placed his empty glass on the nightstand, overcome with a sudden tiredness. The room was spinning. He tried to stand but stumbled. Astrid jumped up and eased him onto the mattress so that he was laying across the bedspread. She took a pillow and propped it under his head.

"That's it," she said in a cooing voice. "I think it's time you slept now."

"What's happening to me?" Decker asked, but the words came out slurred and unintelligible.

"Hush." Astrid leaned over and placed a finger on his lips, a momentary touch. She reached into his pocket and removed the cell phone Adam Hunt had given him, then picked up the wine bottle and left the room.

FORTY-NINE

BRIGHT MORNING SUNLIGHT was streaming into the room when Decker awoke. He opened his eyes and groaned, a headache splitting his skull. What had Astrid done to him? He remembered their conversation about contacting CUSP, and her showing up at his room scantily clad with a bottle of wine. She'd cajoled him into sharing a drink even though he'd rebuked her advances. It was clear now that she had an ulterior motive. It was also clear that he'd been drugged.

Decker forced his legs off the bed and stood up, reaching out to steady himself as a wave of dizziness hit. The bathrobe Astrid had discarded the night before was still laying on the floor, untouched. He kicked it out of the way, stumbled to the bathroom, and splashed water on his face. Back in the bedroom, he changed his shirt and grabbed a jacket, before heading out into the corridor and making his way to Astrid's room. He pounded on the door, but harbored little hope that she was still there.

"What are you doing?" Harry stood at the foot of the third-floor stairs, a quizzical look on his face.

"I'm looking for Astrid. Have you seen her?"

"Not since we last spoke," Harry said.

"Do you have a key to this door?" Decker asked.

"Sure. But I can't use it. There is such a thing as privacy you know."

"For God's sake, man," Decker snapped. "The woman drugged me last night. If you don't open this door, I'll kick it down myself."

"Okay. Calm down." Harry reached into his pocket and took out a key ring loaded with keys. He crossed to the door and unlocked it. "If anyone asks, I didn't let you in."

"I can't imagine who would ask." Decker pushed the door open and stepped inside. The curtains were drawn, swathing the space in darkness. Decker went to the window and opened them.

Light spilled into the room.

Astrid's bed had not been slept in. The nightstand was devoid of personal items. The wardrobe contained nothing but empty clothes hangers. The only sign she had ever been there were the broken open halves of two capsules, a few grains of the white powder they contained spilled around them. Prescription sleeping pills, no doubt. This was how she'd drugged him, lacing his glass prior to pouring the wine.

He stepped back into the corridor.

Harry lingered, watching Decker's every move. "I must say, I'm a little surprised the sergeant hasn't returned to arrest you."

"Me too." Decker was already heading for the stairs. He descended, hurried through the bar, and exited the pub via the side door. A few minutes later, he arrived at the Garda station.

Here, he paused.

If the sergeant was here he might end up in the cells. But what other choice did he have? Astrid had taken his phone, and had surely lied about sending an email to CUSP. There was no outside help coming. His only chance lay in convincing the sergeant to release Hunt. This assumed the policeman was even inside. His police car was not there and Decker was still a free man, which would indicate that the sergeant was otherwise engaged.

Decker gripped the handle and pushed the door open. He peered inside, seeing right away that Sergeant Byrne was not in the Garda station. He hurried through the station to the cells.

"Hunt? Colum?" Decker shouted out. "Rory?"

"In here." Hunt's voice drifted from beyond the locked door of the closest cell.

Decker drew back the panel covering the viewing slot set into the door. He looked inside to see his friends perched in a row on a concrete ledge at the back of the small room. "Am I glad to see you," he said.

"Me too." Hunt stood and approached the door. "I don't suppose you would let us out?"

"Hang on." Decker returned to the main office and scoured it for the cell keys. He didn't find them. He returned to the cell. "No luck."

"My phone is on Byrne's desk," Hunt said. "Bring it to me. I'll call CUSP and end this. I've had enough."

Decker glanced back into the main office. "There's no phone."

"It must be there. Byrne put my phone and the Land Rover keys on the desk before he threw me in here. I saw him."

"Well, it's not there now. Neither are the Land Rover keys," Decker said. "The sergeant must have taken them with him. Where is he anyway?"

"Beats me." Hunt was pacing back and forth in the confined space now.

Colum spoke up. "He threw me and Rory in the cell along with Hunt, and took our phones too. Then he took off like his arse was on fire."

"Someone came in here at around 4 o'clock," Hunt said. "I called out, but didn't get an answer. Then they left again a few moments later."

"Astrid." Decker grimaced. "I bet *she* took the keys and phone."

"Why?" Hunt sounded confused. "What possible reason

could she have to come in here like that without identifying herself?"

"She isn't who you think she is." Decker's head still hurt, but the headache was receding now. "She came to my room after we returned to the Claddagh last night. She drugged me and stole my phone. When I woke up this morning there was no sign of her."

"That makes no sense," Hunt said.

"It does if she's working for someone else," Decker replied.

"Impossible. We vetted her." Hunt shook his head. "Our processes are stringent."

"Impossible or not, she did it."

"You need to find the sergeant so that we can get out of here." Hunt stopped pacing and approached the door again. He peered through the slot. "And then we'll find Astrid and deal with her."

"The last time I saw the sergeant, he was on his way back to the monastery," Decker said.

"Makes sense. When he discovered you and Astrid missing, he became quite annoyed. He thought you were still in the caves."

"Hang tight," Decker said. "I'll get you out."

"Good." Hunt noted. "And if you happen to come across Astrid along the way, do whatever is necessary, and don't bother being nice."

FIFTY

WHEN DECKER ARRIVED BACK at the Claddagh Arms Harry was behind the bar preparing to open up for the day. When he saw Decker enter, he stopped what he was doing.

"You had no luck at the Garda station, I take it?" He said, wringing out the cloth he'd been wiping the bar down with into a sink and then discarding it.

"Byrne wasn't there." Decker crossed to the bar. "He never returned last night after putting Colum and Rory in the cells. My guess is that he's still up at the monastery."

"Why would he still be there?" Harry raised an eyebrow.

"That's a very good question." Decker decided that it was about time that Harry told the truth. "There's something going on in this village, and you know what it is. Tell me."

"I have no idea what you're talking about." Harry shook his head and turned his back on Decker, pulling wine bottles out of a box and placing them on the shelf behind the bar.

"You're lying." Decker went to the bar hatch and slipped behind the counter. He approached the landlord with grim determination. "Your sergeant is missing. My friends are locked in a cell for no good reason. Astrid is gone, and presumably up to no good. I'm trying to be a nice guy here, but my patience is wearing thin, and I don't have time to pussyfoot around. Start talking."

"Okay, okay. Easy there." Harry backed away, the look on his face betraying his unease at Decker's implied threat. "I don't know where to begin. This is going to sound crazy. You won't believe me."

"You'd be surprised at what I'll believe," Decker said. "Tell me."

"There something living under the village. A creature. It's been there for as long as anyone can remember." Harry stopped talking, as if the words sounded crazy even to him.

"A creature." Decker's suspicions were confirmed. This was why Adam Hunt had wanted him along on this job. "What kind of creature?"

"An ancient beast brought here by the Danes. It's been living in the caves for centuries. An ogre."

"Grendel." Decker watched the landlord's reaction as he said the word and knew that he was correct.

Harry hung his head low. "Yes."

"And you didn't think it was worth warning us about this before now?" Decker felt his anger rising. Harry and the rest of the people in this village had put their lives in danger by withholding pertinent information. "You let us go down into those caves under the monastery knowing that a dangerous beast was down there? For goodness sake, Robert and Astrid have been here for weeks excavating. Robert might still be alive if you had mentioned this sooner."

"We had no idea that they would stumble upon caves under the monastery. There were always rumors that the labyrinth extended under the ruins, but no one had ever found anything."

"Did you even look?"

Harry remained silent.

"I'll take that as a no," Decker said. "But that doesn't matter right now. We need to find the sergeant and get my friends out of that cell so that we can deal with Astrid."

"If Sergeant Byrne's still up the monastery, that's a problem," Harry replied. "I'm going to call in some help on this."

"Who?"

"Sean O'Mara. He knows as much about Grendel as anyone in the village. He also has a shotgun, and I think a weapon might come in useful." Harry was already dialing a number on his cell phone. After a brief conversation he hung up. "He'll be here soon."

Decker nodded and walked back around to the front side of the bar. He perched on a stool and watched the bartender fuss around in a clear attempt to divert his nervous energy. A few minutes later the pub door opened, and Sean O'Mara entered, a grim expression on his face.

"This situation is getting out of hand," he said, approaching the bar. "First Craig, then Father Cleary, and now the sergeant is missing too."

"What do you mean?" Harry looked shocked. "Something's happened to Father Cleary?"

"He's dead," Sean said the words in a matter of fact way. "At least, as far as we know. Molly and Gladys found his blood all over the church yesterday. It looks like Grendel has been getting out of the caves. Byrne had me put a padlock on a door under the monastery to keep him in." Sean narrowed his eyes and glared at Decker. "And to keep you people out."

"Yeah, well, you failed on both counts." Decker stood up. "That padlock didn't keep Grendel in, and I assume Astrid is up at the caves as we speak."

"As is Sergeant Byrne," Harry said.

"We'd better be off to find him then," Sean said. He glared at Decker. "None of this would be happening if it wasn't for you people, you know that, right?"

"None of this would be happening if you'd been truthful

with us from the start," Decker replied, moving off toward the door. "But the finger-pointing can wait. Time's wasting, and the longer we take, the less chance we have of finding your sergeant in one piece and getting my friends out of that cell."

FIFTY-ONE

THEY DROVE up to the monastery in Sean's van. Their suspicion that Sergeant Byrne hadn't left the caves was confirmed upon arrival. His police car was parked next to the Land Rover. Flashlights in hand, Decker and Harry exited the van and were about to set off toward the ruins when Sean stopped them.

"Hang on a minute," Sean said, going to the rear of the van and opening the double doors. He rummaged around inside, pushing a toolbox out of the way, and then returned to them carrying three cans of spray paint. "I bought these last week to paint the railings outside St. Ignatius. Haven't gotten around to doing the job yet, and a good thing too. One for each of us."

"Why in God's name would we want spray paint?" Harry asked. "I want to find the sergeant, not get arrested for vandalism."

"The caves are a maze. They stretch for miles," Sean replied.

"We can use the paint to mark our way, so that we don't get lost." Decker slapped Sean on the back. "Good thinking."

They set off through the ruins to the crypt entrance. Here they paused. Sean and Harry looked down into the hole with trepidation.

"It's hard to believe that the caves stretch all this way." Sean aimed his flashlight into the hole in the ground, the beam playing across the winding stone steps.

"Are you sure that going down there is a smart idea?" Harry glanced toward Decker. "The village has spent hundreds of years watching over Grendel, and now we're going to wander around the very place where we kept him locked up. What if we run into trouble?"

"We don't have a choice," Decker said. "Your sergeant is down there. Don't you want to find him?"

"Well, I'm not going first." Harry folded his arms, a defiant look on his face.

"I'll go first." Decker aimed his flashlight into the hole and started down, following the stone steps into the darkness under the monastery. Behind him, following along at a distance, came Sean. Harry went last.

When they were all in the crypt, Decker led them toward the inner room, and the door carved with demons.

Sean glanced around nervously. "I can't believe I'm doing this. I must be feckin crazy."

"You and me both," grumbled Harry. "If it wasn't for the amount of beer the sergeant packs away, I'd let him stay down here. Don't let anyone say I don't go the extra mile for my customers."

"It's not just Sergeant Byrne," Decker said as they stepped past the door into the caves. "Astrid could be down here somewhere too, although what her objective is, I have no idea. Suffice to say that we need to be careful. Her recent actions would indicate that she's dangerous."

"I still can't believe that she drugged you," Harry said. "She was so nice and polite."

"That archaeologist woman dosed you?" Sean cast a sideways glance at Decker. "How did that happen?"

"I'd rather not talk about it." Decker pressed ahead. They were passing through the bone field now. The disarticulated remains of several bodies poked up through the dusty earth of the cave floor. Several vertebrae lay in a curving S shape like some kind of skeletal snake, the rest of the corpse either carried off or scattered. A cracked and broken skull watched them with dead, empty sockets.

When he saw the remains scattered around the floor, Harry balked. "Sweet mother of God, you've led us into hell."

"I guess we've found Grendel's old dining room." Sean hurried past the bones, careful not to crush any underfoot. "There are stories that the monks used to sacrifice themselves to him way back before the monastery fell. I guess they're all true."

"This place is giving me the heebie-jeebies." Harry raced through the bone field and continued on without looking back. "I sure hope we don't end up as a pile of bones down here too."

"Our best bet to avoid that is to find Byrne and beat a hasty retreat." Decker was aware that Hunt, Rory, and Colum were still locked up in the Clareconnell police station. When they found the sergeant, they would also find the keys to the cell door. If they failed to locate the policeman, Decker would be forced to waste valuable time getting the door open by other means. That would give Astrid an even bigger head start. Assuming she hadn't fallen prey to Grendel, herself, that was.

They had reached the cavern where Robert died now. To his left Decker could make out the edge of the chasm and he gave it a wide berth. This was as deep as he had ventured into the caves on any of his previous excursions and now, he was presented with a dilemma. On the far side of the cavern yawned the entrances to a pair of unexplored tunnels. One or both of these, he reasoned, must run for many miles all the way back to the village and they surely branched off into other caves that ran deeper underground. He came to an uncomfortable decision. They didn't have the time to explore each of them as a group. That meant they must split up, and he said as much.

"You're kidding, right?" Harry was alarmed. "Splitting up seems like the worst thing we could do."

"We don't have a choice." Decker didn't like the idea any more than Harry did. "We'll cover more ground if we split up though. I'll take the left-hand cave. The pair of you take the other cave. We have the paint cans. Make a mark every ten feet and if you enter another tunnel spray an arrow so that you know which way is out."

"This is a terrible idea," Sean said, but even so he moved off toward the tunnel.

"Check your watches. We'll meet back here in an hour." Decker stepped toward the right-hand cave, then glanced back toward the two men, before stepping into the unknown.

FIFTY-TWO

DECKER MADE his way into the tunnel, the darkness enveloping him like a shroud. Only his flashlight beam, which he played across the floor and walls ahead, provided a meager amount of light. He pushed deeper, pausing every so often to paint an arrow in the direction of the exit.

There was no sign of Sergeant Byrne so far. The caves were a maze and the policeman had been in them all night. He could be anywhere. He might also have stumbled and fallen into a chasm, just like Robert had. If that were the case, they might never find him. This thought did little to comfort Decker as he pressed on.

Soon he came to a fork, the cave meandering off in different directions. He stopped and listened, but only silence greeted his ears. He shined the flashlight down both tunnels but did not see anything that made one a better pick than the other. In the end he turned to the left and followed a narrow cleft that sloped down into the bowels of the earth, steep rock walls pressing in on both sides. Even though he didn't suffer from claustrophobia, Decker fought an overwhelming urge to turn and flee back to the surface. He pushed the feeling aside and pressed forward with grim determination.

Then he smelled it. A rancid, pungent odor that Decker knew all too well.

The scent of death.

It wafted on the currents of chill air that moved through the caves, heavy and cloying. It stung his nose and caught in the back of his throat. Decker slowed, moving ahead with caution now, his senses on high alert. Up ahead, the tunnel widened into a cavern even larger than the one he'd come from, and there on the floor, caught in the beam of his flashlight, a human arm, the skin and muscle ripped away to reveal white bone underneath.

Decker drew in a sharp breath. He exited the tunnel and swung the flashlight around, hardly able to believe what he was seeing.

Bodies.

Corpses everywhere in all states of decomposition. Many were mere skeletons, but others, those at the top of the heap, looked fresh. The stench here was unbelievable. Decker gagged and fought back the urge to vomit. He staggered back a few steps and put his hand out to steady himself against the tunnel wall. If Sergeant Byrne was in here, he was dead.

Across the floor, on the other side of the cavern, Decker could see another tunnel leading off into blackness. He saw something else too. A shape crouched near the tunnel entrance, manlike yet animalistic, and in its arms, a severed human head.

Decker stared in horror, trying to make sense of what he was seeing. He wanted to run but could not tear his eyes away from the hideous sight. He lifted the flashlight to get a better look, and as the beam hit the creature's face it recoiled and gave a guttural deep-throated hiss. It dropped the head and stood up, meeting Decker's gaze. Then it lumbered forward, out of the flashlight's beam, directly toward Decker.

"Grendel, no!" The voice came from behind Decker. He recognized it instantly. Astrid.

He turned, caught in a moment of confusion, just as she swung at him. He lifted his arms to fend off the unexpected attack, but not fast enough. His Skull exploded in a cacophony of pain. Burning embers of silvery light danced behind his eyes. He felt himself losing the battle to stay on his feet. He tottered a moment, reaching out toward the cave wall, then crumpled to the floor as darkness flickered at the edges of his vision. As unconsciousness rushed in, he saw Astrid hold out her arms, a smile on her face, and beckon to the beast…

FIFTY-THREE

HARRY AND SEAN were deep in the caves, navigating a tight and steeply dropping shaft when they decided to turn back. They had followed winding tunnels for the last thirty minutes without a sign of Sergeant Byrne. Sean checked his watch at intervals, eager to be above ground again. Now they followed their hastily scrawled spray marks back through the maze of shafts and tunnels toward the cavernous vault of rock where they had split up in the first place. With any luck, Sean thought, the American would already be there waiting for them. At this point he didn't even care if Sergeant Byrne was also waiting. He just wanted to escape the darkness, and the monster he knew lurked within it.

"This is a waste of time, if you ask me," Harry said, scowling, as they reached one of the many places where the tunnels had split and followed their sprayed arrow into the left-hand shaft. "Tromping around in the darkness, looking for Byrne. I don't know how that Yank talked us into this. The sergeant's probably dead and we both know it."

"We don't know any such thing," Sean replied as they walked, one behind the other, through a particularly narrow section of tunnel. "Besides, he'd do the same for you."

"I'm not so sure about that." Harry scampered to walk alongside Sean again as the tunnel widened. His flashlight beam played across the walls, searching for the sprayed markers that would lead them back to safety. "The man's spineless, and we both know it."

"He was brave enough to come down here on his own last night," Sean said. "I'm not sure I'd want to venture into these caves after dark."

"The only reason he would've come down here is if he thought Grendel was somewhere else."

"Which makes him smarter than us," Sean observed. They were almost back to the cavern where they had split up in the first place. Up ahead, the entrance yawned, and beyond that, a flat expanse broken only by the thrusting columns of stalagmites reaching for their counterparts hanging from the cave's ceiling above. He hurried his step and was almost back to the cavern when he came to a halt.

"Why are you stopping?" Harry asked.

"Quiet. I thought I heard a voice."

"It's probably the American, Decker, and the sergeant," Harry said.

"I don't think so. It sounded like a woman."

"Astrid?"

"Maybe. Keep it down. I don't want them to hear us." Sean flattened himself against the wall near the cave entrance. He turned his flashlight off and motioned for Harry to do the same.

Darkness swam in around them.

From somewhere in the main cavern, Sean saw a beam of light appear. Moments later, two figures came into view. He recognized one as Astrid. Beside her, loping along, was Grendel.

He heard Harry draw in a sharp breath and nudged him to stay silent.

Astrid and Grendel crossed through the cavern in the direction of the crypt. As they walked, she spoke to him in a soft, lilting voice. Grendel, for his part, reciprocated with a series of low mewing grunts. Then they were gone, swallowed up by the tunnel on the far side of the cavern.

Sean waited a while and then clicked his flashlight back on. He realized he'd been holding his breath, and released the air in a slow, drawn-out exhalation.

Harry turned his own light on. "Sweet Jesus, did you see that?"

"Yeah." Sean peered into the cavern, then took a tentative step from the tunnel. "I did."

"He was walking along with her like some kind of pet." Harry shuddered and followed Sean. "That was messed up."

"She came from the same cave Decker entered."

"You think he ran into her?"

"I don't know," Sean said. If they had encountered each other it was unlikely that Decker fared well, given Astrid's monstrous companion. "I hope not."

"What are we going to do?"

"We stay put." Sean glanced toward the cave leading back to the crypt, which Astrid and Grendel had entered minutes before. It would be foolhardy to attempt a return to the surface right now, with the beast so close at hand. "We wait a while and hope that Decker isn't dead."

FIFTY-FOUR

DECKER AWOKE IN TOTAL DARKNESS.

He lifted a hand and touched the side of his head, wincing at the resulting stab of pain. When he brought the hand away it felt sticky. Blood. He sat up and felt around, hoping to find the flashlight, but saw only swirling blackness. Either the light had broken when he fell, or Astrid had taken it. He reached out and fumbled blindly, praying that the flashlight would be close by. Instead his hand touched a cold and hard object—not what he was looking for. He picked it up anyway, realizing it was the crowbar Hunt had brought to pry the door open the previous day. They had left it at the cave entrance. Astrid must have found it upon her return to the caves and then wielded it to render him unconscious.

Of the flashlight, there was no sign.

Decker struggled to his feet and felt around until he found the entrance to the tunnel from which he had emerged. He gripped the crowbar in one hand and edged forward, following the wall with the other hand. Astrid, he reasoned, was probably long gone, but the crowbar made him feel safer. Especially since he was, effectively, blind. It had taken him almost half an hour to reach the cavern stacked with corpses. Grendel's lair. It would take exponentially longer to find his way back to the original point of entry, especially since he could not see the spray marks indicating which direction to go. This presented a problem. The caves were rambling, and one wrong turn would send him stumbling deeper into the labyrinth rather than back to safety. He stopped and pondered this. There were two choices. He could either keep going and attempt to find his way back in the dark – by no means, an easy task – or he could stay where he was and hope that Sean and Harry came looking for him. The latter course of action assumed that the two men actually realized that he was in trouble. It also relied upon them not having run into Astrid and Grendel, because if they had, they may not be alive to render any assistance. Astrid had stopped Grendel from attacking Decker even as she pressed her own assault, but there was no guarantee that she would restrain the beast again. Decker was unsure why she had even bothered to halt Grendel's attack on him. She certainly had no compunction using the crowbar, which could just as easily have been lethal. Perhaps she genuinely felt some small connection to Decker after their shared experiences, or maybe she just didn't want to waste the time it would have taken for Grendel to rip him apart. Decker was unsure which to believe but leaned toward her simply wishing to make a quick escape. Regardless of Astrid's motivations, there was a choice to be made if he wished to stay alive and neither of the alternatives was great. After weighing his options, Decker concluded that he must forge ahead regardless of the risk.

He inched forward, using the cave wall as a guide. The blackness played tricks on his eyes, and more than once he thought he saw something move. Each time he stopped, heart pounding in his chest, and each time it turned out to be his imagination. He fought a rising panic that surged up from deep inside his mind. Were these cold, unyielding caves going to be his tomb? He pushed the terror away, gulped it back down. He would need to keep a cool head to stay alive.

He carried on, lurching along like a blind man. At one point his foot caught on a jutting rock and he toppled, throwing his hands forward to break his fall and landing on his knees. The rough ground scraped his shins even through his jeans. He struggled back up, grateful not to have broken any bones, and resumed his torturous journey. Every so often, he stopped and listened, hoping to hear Harry or Sean, but only silence rang in his ears.

Then, just as he was starting to think that it was hopeless, he saw a faint glow in the tunnel ahead, getting brighter.

His heart leapt.

A flashlight. Someone had found him.

He opened his mouth to call out then thought better of it. What if Astrid and Grendel were returning to the charnel house Decker had just escaped? He stood a moment, frozen in indecision. If he stayed here, he would be discovered for sure, but the only other option was to return to Grendel's lair and onward through the cave he'd seen at the other side. That would be no mean feat considering that he could not see where he was going. Not only that, but he would be moving in the wrong direction and could, potentially, end up hopelessly lost. Neither option was good. He did, however, have the crowbar. It was not a great weapon, but it did provide a means to defend himself, and Astrid might not realize that he was armed. This gave him an advantage, albeit slim. Standing his ground, Decker surmised, was the best option if he hoped to escape the caves. He gripped the crowbar tight and waited.

The flashlight's beam was getting brighter now, its owner drawing near. It swept across the walls and floor, and then, found Decker.

He squinted as the light caught his face. The sudden brightness rendered him as blind as the darkness had previously. He could not tell who was behind the light, but then he heard a familiar voice.

"Decker?"

"Sergeant Byrne." Relief flooded over Decker. It wasn't

Astrid and Grendel who had found him, but the very person they had entered the caves to look for in the first place.

"Am I glad to see you. I've been lost in these tunnels for hours." Byrne lowered the flashlight as he approached Decker. "Where's Astrid?"

"That's a long story." Decker started forward, closing the gap between them. "Have you seen Harry and Sean?"

"They're down here too?"

"We split up. We were looking for you."

"Do you know how to get out of here?" There was a tinge of hope in the sergeant's voice.

"Shine the flashlight along the wall," Decker instructed him. "You should see arrows sprayed there. That's our way out."

Sergeant Byrne did as he was told and grinned. "Well I'll be darned. I suppose it would be rude of me to arrest you now, under the circumstances."

"I rather think it would." Decker nodded in the direction of the exit. "What do you say we find the others and get out of here."

"That sounds like a fine idea." Sergeant Byrne started off following the arrows. "I hope I never set foot in these caves again as long as I live."

FIFTY-FIVE

WHEN THEY ARRIVED BACK at the main cavern, Harry and Sean were already waiting. When they saw Decker and the sergeant they rushed forward with exclamations of relief.

"We thought Grendel had killed you guys." Sean slapped Decker heartily on the back. "We almost ran into him ourselves."

"And Astrid too," Harry said. "They came through here like they were out for a Sunday stroll in the park."

"Astrid and Grendel are together?" Sergeant Byrne looked confused. "That doesn't make any sense."

"A lot has happened since you went missing," Decker said. "Astrid isn't one of the good guys. I don't know what her game is yet, but she has some sort of hold over the beast."

"She drugged Decker last night after they got back to the pub," Harry said. "You should have seen him this morning, he looked like he'd been on a three-day bender."

"She drugged you?" Sergeant Byrne glanced at Decker. "How did you let that happen?"

"I'll tell you later." Decker started across the cavern toward the tunnel leading to the crypt. "Right now, I think we should get back above ground."

"Suits me." Byrne tagged along behind with the others following.

"And when we get back to Clareconnell you're going to let Adam and the others out of that cell."

"I'll make that decision, thank you very much." The sergeant hurried to keep up with Decker as they entered the tunnel.

"I could just take the keys and leave you down here," Decker said as they picked their way through the mess of scattered bones. "Your choice."

"Okay. No need to get touchy." Byrne glanced at a cracked and yellowed skull, a look of disgust on his face. "I was just making a point."

"Fair enough, but if you want any chance of stopping Grendel before he eats anymore of your villagers, you're going to need Adam Hunt."

"We've managed well enough with Grendel so far," Sergeant Byrne said. "If it wasn't for those damned archaeologists, he'd still be safely locked down here."

"Astrid would have freed him whatever happened," Decker pointed out. "She was working against us, remember? For all we know it was her that killed Robert. When we found her, she claimed she was lost, but my guess is that she was actually looking for Grendel."

"You think it was all an act?" Sergeant Byrne asked. "Her concussion and all that."

"She hasn't been truthful with anything else," Decker replied.

They were approaching the inner door now, beyond which a dark and narrow tunnel made of smooth stone blocks led to the demon door, and the crypt beyond. Decker slowed and motioned for the others to do the same. He peered inside, noting that the door at the end of the tunnel, which they had left open, was now closed. Grendel and Astrid had come this way, and presumably shut it behind them. Decker felt a tingle of foreboding. He led the group into the tunnel, and they continued forward. Moments later, they arrived at the door carved with demons, but when he tried to open it, the door would not move. He tried again, putting more weight into it this time. No luck. The door was locked, trapping them underground.

"Astrid must have drawn the bolt across when she left the caves." Decker lifted the crowbar and pushed it in between the wall and the door. He pulled, grunting with effort. The door didn't move. He swore and repositioned the crowbar then tried again, putting all his might into it.

Sean stepped forward and positioned himself next to Decker, gripping the exposed end of the bar. "Let me help with that."

Together they pulled but succeeded in doing nothing except chipping flakes of the wall away that fell to the earth under their feet.

"This is impossible," Decker said, frustrated. "We're not getting out this way. The door is too sturdy."

"It was built to keep Grendel contained." Sean shook his head. "If a monster with inhuman strength couldn't break through it, there's no way we're going to be able to."

"That's just great," Sergeant Byrne said, his face contorting into a mask of fear. "We're going to die down here."

"Not if I can help it," Decker said. He turned to Sean. "Try your cell phone. See if we can get a signal."

"Good idea." Sean took his phone out and held it up in the darkness. The screen glowed bright. He scowled. "No bars."

"I'll try mine," Byrne said. He held his own phone up then shook his head. "Same here. No service."

"Shit." Sean turned and slammed a fist into the door. "Whatever are we going to do now?"

"There must be another way out of these caves," Decker said. "These types of underground systems always have more than one entrance."

"There is one other way out," Harry replied at length. "The church."

"That's right," Sean said, his voice tinged with hope. "The church. I'd forgotten about that. All we need to do is get there."

"What about the church?" Decker asked.

"There's an entrance under St. Ignatius." Sean leaned against the door. "Since Grendel was able to come and go from the caves right here, the whole system must connect up. All we need to do is find the right tunnel."

"The village is miles away," Harry said. "That's a long way to walk in the dark. One wrong turn and we'll never escape."

"Have you got a better idea?" Sean asked.

"No, I wish I did." Harry stared down at the ground. "I should have stayed in the pub where it was safe."

"We are probably safer down here," Sergeant Byrne said. "Did you forget, Grendel is out there somewhere. God knows what will happen if he reaches the village."

"It's daylight," Decker said. "Grendel isn't going to do anything. At least not until nightfall. He has an aversion to light, don't forget. Besides, my guess is that Astrid has taken the Land Rover and is hightailing it out of the area even as we speak."

"You think?" The sergeant looked incredulous.

"I do," Decker replied. "Which is why we need to find our way out of these caves as quickly as possible and stop her. Even if they leave the village alone, that doesn't make Grendel any less dangerous."

"We'd better get moving then," Sean said. He stepped past the others and began walking back in the direction of the caves. "No point in hanging around here."

"No point at all." Decker motioned to Harry. "After you."

"For the record, I still wish I was back at the pub, Grendel or not." Harry started off along the tunnel.

Decker waited for Sergeant Byrne to move and then followed up the rear. Moments later, they entered the caves for the second time that day…

FIFTY-SIX

THE GROUP RETRACED their steps back to the main cavern, and here they paused, confronted by the two cave entrances that had necessitated Decker, Harry, and Sean split up to search for Sergeant Byrne in the first place. After a brief conversation they decided that the left-hand tunnel, the one Decker had originally taken, would be their best bet, since that was where Grendel's lair was located. It was unlikely that Grendel had made his home in such a place unless it was close to the church entrance, since all contact between Grendel and the villagers had, up until now, occurred there.

With their route decided, the group set off once more, navigating the tight and claustrophobic tunnels. They followed Decker's spray marks in reverse and soon found themselves at Grendel's charnel house.

They came to a stop at the entrance and steeled themselves for the journey through the grotesque and alarming space.

"Of all that's holy, I think we are standing at the rim of hell," Harry said, peering at the mounds of stacked bodies. "There must be hundreds of corpses here."

"Grendel's been locked up for almost a thousand years,"

Sean replied. "He must've been bringing his victims back here for centuries."

"Because it's close to the church, I'll wager." Harry sounded hopeful, although Decker could tell that he didn't relish the idea of navigating the corpse-strewn cave. "We might actually get out of this alive."

"Why would Grendel need to be close to the church?" Decker asked, sensing that he was missing a vital piece of information.

The three Clareconnell men shared guarded looks, and then Harry shrugged. "A hunch, that's all."

"We should keep moving," Byrne said stepping into the cave and picking his way along through a narrow path between the piles of bodies. "I want to put this house of horrors behind us."

Decker followed along, his suspicions aroused, but willing to ignore them for now, for the sake of putting distance between himself and the cave. Behind him, Sean and Harry huddled close. Then, when they were halfway through, Decker realized that the two men had stopped. He turned to find Sean kneeling on the path next to a freshly discarded corpse.

There were tears in his eyes. He looked up as the other men formed a circle around him. "Craig," he mumbled through clenched teeth. "Grendel killed him."

"We suspected that already," Harry placed a reassuring hand on Sean's shoulder. "Come on mate, there's nothing you can do for him now."

"Leave me alone." Sean pushed Harry away and bent low cradling Craig's head in his arms. He reached out and closed his friend's eyes, then laid the body gently back on the ground. He hunched over, rocking back and forth. "I'm so sorry," he mumbled. "I'm sorry for everything."

"We need to go," Byrne said, after a minute passed. "We'll come back for him when this is over."

Sean stayed kneeling a few seconds longer, staring down at his friend's ruined body, then he stood and turned to Decker.

"You're going to stop Grendel, right? You'll make sure he never hurts anyone again?"

"Yes." Decker nodded. "You have my word."

"Good." Sean cast one last glance at his friend, and then strode past the gathered men in the direction of the unknown tunnel on the other side of the cavern.

Decker set off with Harry and Aiden Byrne at his side.

As they walked, the landlord leaned in close to the Byrne. "It wasn't just Craig back there," he said. "I saw Barry Clamaugh and his wife. They were all ripped to pieces."

"I know," the sergeant replied. "Father Cleary was there too, but I tried not to look at him."

They stepped into the tunnel.

Decker was relieved to be out of the corpse field, but soon it became apparent that they were not out of danger. Within five minutes of entering the tunnel they reached a fork with caves that meandered off in wildly different directions.

Once more, they stopped.

"This is getting ridiculous," Harry mumbled. "I'm starting to wish that Grendel was here, so that he could show us the way out."

"Maybe he can," Decker said, studying the ground in front of them. Because there, in the loose sand that covered the cave floor, was the clear impression of a foot. "We follow the footprints."

"That's the first time I've ever been glad for Grendel," Sean said.

They started to walk, scanning the ground ahead of them. The footprints continued on for what Decker estimated must've been at least half a mile, leading them first left, and then right, then left once again through multiple splitting tunnels, before finally petering out as the ground changed from loose shingle and sand, to hard smooth rock.

Decker's heart sank. If the tunnels split now, they would have no clue which direction to take. Then, up ahead, Byrne's flashlight beam picked out a flat vertical surface blocking their path. At first, Decker had no idea what he was looking at, but then it dawned on him.

A trap door made of stone.

This must be the entrance under St. Ignatius.

As if to prove him right, Sean let out a whoop of joy. "We made it."

"Thank heavens for that," Harry said. "I was beginning to think we'd never find it."

As one, they hurried their step and reached the door.

Then a new problem presented itself.

The door, short and squat at only four feet tall, sat in vertical grooves set into the tunnel's side walls. On the ceiling above the door, one on each side near the walls, hung a pair of pulleys. A double rope emerged from a small hole near the ceiling and split to the left and right, running across the pulleys and down to a pair of U-shaped metal fixings set into the top lip of the door itself. The bottom of the door sat in a deep groove within the floor.

Sergeant Byrne placed his hands on the door and felt around, looking for purchase. He knelt and ran his fingers along the groove where the door met the floor. Unable to find a handhold, he stood up, a concerned look on his face, and leaned against the cave wall. "This is no better than the door under the monastery."

Decker stepped up to the door and examined it, coming to the same conclusion as the sergeant. There was no way to lift the door.

They were trapped.

FIFTY-SEVEN

DECKER and the rest of the group stood, crestfallen, at the sturdy trap door that blocked their path to freedom.

"How do we get it open?" Harry asked, his eyes wide with fear.

"We don't," Sean replied bitterly. "The damned thing's meant to keep Grendel at bay, and it's been doing a fine job of it for hundreds of years. If Grendel couldn't lift the door, we sure as hell aren't going to be able to. And even if we could, it won't matter. There's another door in our way, and that one's locked too. I know, because I locked it myself."

"Actually, it's not locked," Byrne said.

"What?" Sean looked startled. "How is that?"

"I came down here to investigate after Father Cleary disappeared. I opened that door. Unless someone has been down since, it should still be open."

"Heavens. You might just have saved all our lives," Harry said.

"Except that we still can't get past this first door," Sean replied.

"What about the ropes?" Harry eyed the pulley contraption. "Can we lift it with those?"

"Not a chance." Sean shook his head. "If we were on the other side of the door it would be easy. It's meant to be opened that way. But there's no leverage from this side, and the door is too heavy for us to pull it up by lifting the ropes alone."

"It gets worse, boys." Sergeant Byrne was holding his phone up near the door. "I thought we might get a signal since we are right underneath the village, but there's still nothing."

"There's a lot of rock between us and the surface, not to mention the church itself," Decker said. "Even if we were sitting right under a cell tower you wouldn't get a signal down here."

"It's better than doing nothing."

"We need to find another exit," Harry said.

"If there's another way out of the caves Grendel never found it in a thousand years." Sean sank to the floor and sat with his back against the cave wall. "We aren't going to come across it in the short time before we starve to death."

"It's a little early to give up, don't you think?" Decker said. He stepped up to the door, gripping the crowbar in both hands, and inserted it into the groove where the door met the floor. He moved the crowbar back and forth, working it into the groove as deep as he could. That done, he pushed down with a grunt, using the lip of the groove as a fulcrum. The tip of the crowbar bit into the hard surface of the door and Decker thought, just for a second, that he felt some give. Then the crowbar slipped and jumped out of the groove crushing Decker's knuckles against the floor.

He cried out in pain and almost dropped the crowbar, but then went back to it, pushing the tool back into the groove and repeating the process. This time he felt a definite movement, but the door was too heavy. Decker cursed and was about to with-draw the crowbar when Sean got to his feet and hurried over to him.

"Here, let me help." Sean stood opposite Decker and gripped the end of the crowbar.

Together they applied downward pressure until, as if by a miracle, the door inched upward with a grinding squeal.

"It's working," Sean exclaimed.

The crowbar slipped deeper into the groove as the door rose ponderously upward. Decker's muscles screamed and a bead of sweat worked its way down his forehead into his eye, stinging. He looked up at Sergeant Byrne and Harry, who were lingering nearby and watching hopefully. "Don't just stand there. Get your fingers in the gap under the door and start lifting."

"What if the crowbar slips?" Sergeant Byrne asked. "The door will crush them."

"That's a risk you're going to have to take," Decker said in a strained voice. "If you don't, the door will definitely slip back and then we'll never get it to open. We were lucky to get it to move this time."

"I don't know," Harry said.

"Just do it." Sean snapped to the two men. His face was red, Jaws clenched with effort.

Byrne sidestepped Sean and reached down.

Harry hesitated a moment, fear flickering in his eyes, but then he took up a position to Decker's left and slipped his fingers into the crack between the door and the floor.

"On three," Decker said. He counted down quickly and then as he reached the number one, all four of them braced. Decker and Sean put as much pressure as they could muster on the crowbar. Harry and Sergeant Byrne puffed and panted as they put their backs into lifting with all their might.

Inch by inch the door lifted at a torturous pace.

"Keep going." Decker could feel the crowbar reaching its maximum leverage. He pushed it further under the door, then once it was useless, he slipped his own hands into the crack and lifted manually.

Sean joined him and now the gap grew wider.

Decker thought his muscles would explode with the exertion,

but then, thankfully the door lifted enough to allow them to escape.

"Hold the door, don't let it drop." Decker reached down and grabbed the crowbar. He scooted around Harry and wedged it vertically against the wall in the gap between the floor and the door.

"Can we let go yet?" Sean asked. "It's damned heavy."

"Yes," Decker held the crowbar steady and prayed that it wouldn't slip and crush his hand. "You can let the door go, but do it together, and quickly."

The three men released their grip and jumped back. Decker tensed as the heavy slab of stone settled, with the crowbar taking its weight. He stepped away and turned to the others.

"We shouldn't wait, I'm not sure how long that crowbar will hold." Decker motioned toward the precariously balanced door. "Someone needs to scoot under that door and use the pulleys to lift it from the other side."

"Not me." Sergeant Byrne looked at the crowbar with distrust.

"It'll take two people to lift that door," Sean said. He dropped to his knees and lowered his head toward the gap, where he hesitated. "I've done it before, so I'll go, but I'll need a second body."

Neither Harry nor Byrne spoke.

"That'll be me then," Decker said. "Let's get this over with."

"Right." Sean dropped to his knees. "I sure hope this doesn't collapse on me."

"You're not the only one," Decker said, preparing himself to follow right behind Sean.

"Here goes nothing." Sean scrambled forward and ducked under the door, careful not to touch it lest he disturb the crowbar. His head disappeared, followed by his torso and finally all that was left was a pair of legs that swiftly scrabbled free. His voice drifted from the other side. "I'm through."

"I guess it's my turn," Decker said. He took a deep breath,

glanced at the crowbar, which was still holding, although at more of an angle now. There wasn't much time. It might give way at any moment. He crawled forward, flattening himself to fit through the narrow gap, then inched along using his elbows. His head passed through, followed by his shoulders. From the other side, Sean reached down and took Decker's arms to assist him.

It was then that Decker noticed the door tremble.

The crowbar started to move. The door dropped an inch lower in its grooves.

Sean cried out, a look of terror on his face.

And then, before Decker had time to react, the crowbar gave way and the door crashed down.

FIFTY-EIGHT

DECKER FELT a whoosh of air as the door plummeted toward him, threatening to crush his legs under its immense weight. Then he was being dragged backward, passing through the gap between the falling door and floor, scrambling free just as the door slammed back into place.

Decker lay on his back, gulping in air. He was shaking. A millisecond longer and he would have been dead.

He let Sean help him to his feet.

"That was a close one," Sean said, a grin cracking his face. "Talk about the luck of the Irish. I think you just used up enough luck for all four of us."

"Next door we come to, I'm going first," Decker said. He brushed himself off and looked around. It was then that he noticed the table sitting in the middle of the room, and the corpse of Tom Walsh laying upon it. He glanced at Sean. "So, this is where all those bodies in Grendel's lair came from."

"It's not what you think." The smile had disappeared from Sean's face now.

"I think it's exactly what I think," Decker said. "You've been feeding Grendel."

"We bring people down here when they pass away," Sean

said. "We leave the bodies for Grendel. I don't like it, but it's better that than the alternative."

"The funeral a few days ago." Decker remembered passing the hearse on his way to the monastery the morning after he arrived in Clareconnell. He remembered something else too. On his walk through the village he'd noticed the absence of a cemetery and mentioned as much to Adam Hunt upon returning to the Claddagh Arms. Now he knew why.

"It's been this way for as long as anyone can remember," Sean said. "Everyone in the village accepts this is what will ultimately happen to them."

Decker felt a wave of revulsion, but he pushed it back down. There were more important issues right now.

From the other side of the door came Sergeant Byrne's voice. "Is everyone okay over there?"

"We're fine," Sean shouted back. "We had a narrow escape, but we're both in one piece."

"Good. Can you let us out please?"

"I've got a good mind to leave them there," Decker said, nodding toward Tom Walsh.

"Then we'll never get your colleagues out of that cell." Sean was already making his way to the other door. He stepped into the corridor and took hold of the rope, then waited for Decker to join him.

Together they heaved.

The rope drew taut.

For a brief second Decker thought the inner door wasn't going to move, but then it started upward at a ponderous rate. Decker's arm muscles screamed for relief and he wondered how the villagers had been doing this for so long without finding a better solution, but then Sean was tying off the rope, and he let go with much relief.

Harry and Aiden Byrne rushed from the caves, clearly glad to be free. When Harry saw the corpse laying on the table, he turned white.

"Not a pleasant sight, huh?" Decker said, stepping back into the offering chamber to meet them. "I knew there was something off with this village."

"It's not our fault," Byrne said, indignant. "We didn't ask for this."

"Really?"

"If you want to blame anyone, how about the ancient Danes. They're the ones who exiled Grendel here." Harry kept his eyes averted from Tom Walsh's corpse. "Or how about the monks who used to sacrifice themselves to it?"

"Their misdeeds don't relieve you of yours," Decker said.

"Guys," Sean stepped between Decker and the sergeant. "Can we play the blame game another time? This isn't a good place to be. We should leave."

"You won't get any argument from me on that," Decker said, moving back toward the chamber's outer door, and the tunnel beyond, which fell away into darkness.

The group left the offering chamber behind and traversed the tunnel. No one spoke. Their ordeal in the caves, and the sight of Tom Walsh's corpse, had left little desire for idle conversation. While Sergeant Byrne and the village at large blamed CUSP and the archeological dig for their current woes, Decker could not help but feel that the residents of Clareconnell had brought Grendel's curse down upon themselves by their own actions. Their refusal to warn the outsiders of the danger lurking in the caves was the ultimate reason why the beast got loose. Astrid's ulterior motives only exacerbated the issue. When he thought about her, Decker felt his anger rising all over again. He only hoped that they would be able to find her and thwart whatever she had planned for Grendel before anyone else died.

At the end of the tunnel another door led into a cold, dank room with a set of stairs at one end. A rusting gurney, no doubt used to transport bodies to and from St. Ignatius, sat idle in the middle of the space.

They hurried to the steps and ascended in single file.

Upon reaching the church, Sean and Harry visibly relaxed. Decker led the group past the Lady Chapel and down the aisle to the doors at the back.

When they stepped out into the daylight Decker turned to the sergeant. "We're going to the police station, right now."

Sergeant Byrne said nothing. He glared at Decker but offered up no argument. They made their way along Winslow Road and soon arrived at the Garda station. After they entered, Decker nudged Byrne toward the cells.

"Let them out," Decker instructed.

Byrne reached into his pocket and took out a set of keys. He looked at Decker. "I should be putting you in the cells right alongside them."

"Really?" Decker took a step toward the sergeant, his eyes narrowing. "Either you open that door, or I'll take those keys from you and do it myself."

"Just do as the man says, Aidan," Sean said. "This is no time to stand on pride."

"Now you're giving me orders too?" Sergeant Byrne's nostrils flared.

"For Pete's sake, just open the door." Harry shook his head. "If it wasn't for Decker, you'd still be down in those caves."

Sergeant Byrne mumbled under his breath but moved toward the door and inserted the key, unlocking it.

He pulled it open.

Adam Hunt, Rory, and Colum were waiting on the other side, arms folded.

"About time," Hunt said. "We were beginning to think you weren't coming back."

"You aren't the only ones," Decker replied. "We barely got out of the caves alive."

"Did you find Astrid?" Hunt stepped out of the cell, shooting Sergeant Byrne a menacing look as he did so.

"We found her alright." Decker waited for Colum and Rory to leave the cell before speaking again. "She took Grendel."

"What?" Rory looked shocked. "She stole the bones?"

"Not exactly," Decker replied. He turned to the sergeant. "You want to tell them?"

"Not really," Byrne admitted. He looked down at the ground.

"Would someone please fill me in?" Hunt snapped. "We don't have all day."

"Grendel is alive," Decker said. "He's been trapped down in the caves for centuries. The villagers have been feeding him."

"You're feckin kidding me," Colum said, his eyes wide. "I knew this town was messed up."

"I guessed as much when we found the door under the monastery busted open." Hunt looked thoughtful. "I assume he was Astrid's true motive for being here all along."

"Looks that way." Sean spoke up. "They just strolled out of the caves together like a pair of old friends. It was creepy."

"She came here last night after drugging me and took the keys to the Land Rover," Decker said. "Which means that she intended to use it for her escape."

"That would appear to be the most logical assumption." Hunt rubbed his chin thoughtfully.

"She and Grendel could be anywhere by now," Harry said. "They have several hours on us."

"Then it's a good job she stole the Land Rover," Hunt replied. "We need to get back to the Claddagh right away."

"Why?" Harry asked.

"You'll see." Hunt was already moving toward the door. "Come along, the more time we waste, the further away they get, and I've had enough of this."

"Can we at least get something to eat before we go chasing after that damned woman?" Colum asked. "I've been in that cell since yesterday evening and I'm starving."

"How can you even think about food at a time like this?" Decker asked.

"It's easy," Colum replied. "Especially when the food we're talking about is one of Harry's all-day breakfasts."

FIFTY-NINE

WHEN THEY ARRIVED BACK at the Claddagh Arms, Harry went directly to the kitchen and whipped them all up a quick meal of sausages, thick-sliced bacon, and eggs, which they ate in grateful silence. Afterward, when the food was gone, Hunt led everyone up to the second-floor bedrooms. Colum unlocked his room and stepped aside to let the group enter. Following them in, he crossed to a chest of drawers and heaved it away from the wall with a grunt.

"What are you doing?" Sergeant Byrne asked.

"Decker called last night from the ruins and told me that you had arrested Adam. I figured you'd be coming for us next and I wanted to make sure you wouldn't find this." Colum knelt and reached behind the chest of drawers and into a space between the furniture and the floor. He withdrew a slim black laptop case then stood up and pushed the drawers back against the wall. "In the light of what has transpired with Astrid, it appears that you weren't the only one I needed to protect this from."

"Tell me you can find her," Hunt said.

"You bet." Colum slipped a laptop out of the case and perched it on the bed. He opened the screen and typed a password in at the prompt. Once in, he clicked on a desktop icon and waited for the software to load.

"You're going to find her using a laptop?" Sergeant Byrne asked, perplexed.

"Sure am." Colum was typing now, moving from screen to screen within the software. He clicked a drop-down box and scrolled until he found an option labeled *Range-Rover–26–A.* "Every CUSP vehicle is equipped with GPS tracking as standard. We can track the Land Rover anywhere around the globe in real-time."

"Wouldn't Astrid know about that?" Sean asked. "She does work for you."

Hunt shook his head. "Astrid and Robert were not part of our organization. We funded the dig at the ruins, but she would be unaware of our greater operational procedures."

"Speaking of which," Sergeant Byrne said. "Who exactly do you guys work for, and don't feed me that UNESCO bull. I don't believe a word of it. There's no way you guys work for the United Nations in any capacity."

"Actually, we do have affiliations with the United Nations," Hunt replied. "And UNESCO will verify our cover story if required, but you are correct. We aren't here to declare the monastery a world heritage site."

"I figured that much out already." Byrne fixed Hunt with a steely gaze. "You still haven't answered my question though."

"We work for an organization called CUSP," Hunt said. "It stands for Classified Universal Special Projects."

"Never heard of it." Byrne looked perplexed. "What does it do exactly?"

"We investigate the unexplained, retrieve unusual objects that could benefit or destroy mankind, and protect humanity from threats the more mainstream government agencies of the world are not equipped to deal with."

"Like some kind of supernatural CIA."

"If you like," Hunt said. He leaned over Colum's shoulder. "Have you found her yet?"

"The Land Rover has stopped moving." Colum pointed to a map within his software. A pulsing round blip indicated the location of the stolen vehicle. "She's about a hundred miles north-west of here. The car has been stationary for almost an hour."

"That's the middle of nowhere," Hunt said. "It looks like there's nothing but empty countryside for miles."

"We need to see what's on the ground there," Decker said, leaning in and peering at the screen.

"I can help with that." Colum clicked off the map. He typed away for a few seconds, and then a new window came up, showing a detailed satellite image of the landscape. "Don't ask me how I'm getting this because I can't tell you. Too many civilians in the room."

Decker studied the image, with a patchwork of fields divided by roads, and the occasional structure dotted across the landscape. "Can you get any closer?"

"What's this?" Colum pecked at the keyboard again. The image zoomed, focusing in on one building in particular. A stone house surrounded by lush green lawns. "Good enough?"

"Impressive," Decker said. The house was large, consisting of a main building with a smaller, one floor wing thrusting from the rear. Another structure standing alone to the right of the main building was, he assumed, a garage. Parked in front of it, plain for all to see, was a vehicle that looked very much like CUSP's stolen Land Rover.

"Brazen." Rory shook his head. "She didn't even bother to park it out of sight."

"That's because she doesn't know that we can do this," Colum replied. He zoomed even closer, confirming the identity of the vehicle, and brought up another screen. He typed away, then looked up at the group. "I have an address for the house."

"Good." Hunt smiled grimly.

"And get this," Colum said. "It's owned by an organization called the Hansen Foundation. Sound familiar?"

"That's Astrid's surname," Rory said. "Are you saying she owns that building?"

"That would be my guess." Colum was busy bringing up more information on the house. "It looks like the property has been owned by the foundation for well over a hundred years. It's one of many such homes dotted around Europe. Denmark, England, France, the list goes on. Some of them date back centuries. There's at least ten houses registered to the Hansen Foundation."

"You're saying Astrid's family own all of those properties?" Sergeant Byrne looked skeptical. "I thought she was just an archaeologist?"

"She might be an archaeologist," Decker said. "But that isn't all she is."

"No, it isn't." Hunt sighed. "She did a good job of covering up her past. I should have seen this before now. It makes perfect sense, why she was so obsessed with Grendel."

"Would someone mind telling me what you're all talking about?" Sergeant Byrne asked.

"Those houses don't belong to Astrid's family," Decker said. "They belong to Astrid herself, and have for centuries."

"Huh?" Byrne glanced between Decker and Hunt.

"What they're trying to say is that Astrid is Grendel's mother." Rory glanced toward the sergeant. "That's why she is so obsessed with finding him. When the Danes took her son away, she must have been heartbroken. She's spent a thousand years searching for him."

"And now that she's found him," Decker said, "Who knows what horrors they will unleash next..."

SIXTY

HUNT PACED BACK and forth in the small bedroom, deep in thought. Eventually he turned back to the group, a grim look upon his face. "We must take care of this situation right now, before Astrid and Grendel make another move and drop off the grid entirely."

"But we already know where they are." Byrne nodded toward Colum's laptop. "I thought you people were part of some powerful government organization. Like super-spies or something. Why don't you just call in the cavalry and take them out?"

"It's not that simple," Hunt said. "We are not the military. We can't just go in guns blazing. We need to stay covert."

"Besides," Colum added. "Our jurisdiction here is tenuous at best. The only way that we could mount a special forces style assault on that mansion would be to let the Irish government know what is going on."

"That would be a containment nightmare," Hunt said. "And even if we could convince the local authorities that a centuries old mother and her cannibalistic ogre of a child are hiding out in that house, they would never let CUSP run the operation. We would be forced to concede our authority and lose the opportunity to capture Grendel for ourselves, dead or alive. Not only that, but it would expose CUSP to unacceptable levels of scrutiny and publicity."

"We have to handle this ourselves." Colum looked up at the group. "There is no other choice."

"I agree." Hunt nodded. He looked around at the expectant group. "It's up to us."

Byrne gave Hunt a nervous look. "You mean you want us to-"

"Heavens, no." Hunt shook his head. "This situation is much too dangerous for civilians. Colum, Decker, Rory, and I will handle it. That's what we do."

"Thank the stars for that." The look of relief on Byrne's face was almost comical. "Is there anything we can do to help you?"

"There is one thing," Hunt said. "We're going to need transportation."

"My car is still parked at the monastery," Sergeant Byrne said.

"Mine too," Sean added. "But I know someone who might be able to help."

"Let's go." Hunt motioned for Sean to lead the way.

Colum closed the laptop and placed it back in the case. Together, they left the bedroom and descended the stairs, through the bar, and out into the street.

Sean led them up the road, and onto a side street until they came to a cottage with a brightly painted yellow door.

"Ellen Hennessey?" The sergeant asked, raising an eyebrow. "Are you sure that's wise?"

"Craig's car is parked right there," Sean nodded toward a Toyota parked at the curb. "Have you got a better idea?"

"We just found her husband's body down in the caves," Byrne said. "She doesn't even know that he's dead yet."

"I know that," Sean said. He approached the front door then turned back to the group. "Craig was my best friend. I should tell her."

Sean paused at the door, then raised his hand and knocked. Two sharp short raps. A moment later the door opened to reveal Ellen Hennessey. She greeted Sean, then her gaze drifted beyond him to Decker and the rest of the group waiting at the curb. Sean spoke to her in a soft voice, the words snatched away by the breeze, and then he stepped inside. The door closed behind him.

They waited, the minutes ticking away. After a quarter of an hour the door opened and Sean emerged. There was no sign of Ellen. He descended the steps and held a set of keys out to Colum.

"Take these," he said.

"How is she?" Sergeant Byrne asked.

"Not good." Sean pushed his hands into his pockets and cast his eyes down toward the ground. "I'm going to stay with her. It's the least that I can do."

Hunt nodded. "Tell her she has our sympathy."

"I'll do that." Sean turned and ascended the steps, then disappeared back into the house, closing the door softly behind him.

"Poor woman," Colum said, his eyes lingering on the door. Then he moved off toward the parked car and unlocked it, slipping behind the wheel.

Hunt turned to Harry and the sergeant. "I shall expect you both to keep everything we've discussed today confidential."

"You have my word," Harry said.

The constable nodded.

"Excellent. We shall be keeping an eye on you to make sure that you do." Hunt turned and approached the car, pulling open the front passenger door. He motioned for Decker and Rory to hop in the back. A moment later they were speeding through the village toward the Irish countryside, and the monster that hid within it.

SIXTY-ONE

THEY DROVE for almost two hours past fields and forests and through small villages dotted across the landscape. Eventually, as the afternoon slipped into evening, they arrived at the house owned by Astrid Hanson. It sat majestic and alone in a field of green, surrounded at the property's boundary by a low stone wall hidden in places by dense bushes and tightly packed trees. A serpentine gravel driveway wound up to the main house. The stolen Land Rover was clearly visible parked near the building's front door. Astrid hadn't even attempted to hide it.

Colum brought their car to a halt at the bottom of the driveway. "What now, boss?" He said, glancing across to Hunt, who occupied the front passenger seat.

"Under normal circumstances I would suggest that we wait until after sundown to approach the house in order to maximize our cover," Hunt replied. "But given Grendel's proclivity for darkness, that is a bad idea. We have no way of knowing if the house has surveillance cameras, or any other means of detecting our approach such as motion sensors, but we must assume that our presence will be noticed whatever we do."

"The minute we approach the building we'll lose the element of surprise," Colum said. "Astrid has owned this property long enough to take advantage of all the security measures available in the modern world, should she be so inclined."

"My thoughts exactly." Hunt peered out the window and across the serene landscape toward the building. "Given the lack of cover, daylight itself becomes our biggest enemy. She won't even need motion sensors to know we're coming. All she'll need to do is merely look out the window."

"We might as well drive up there then," Decker said from the rear. "At least that way we'll have an escape vehicle close at hand, should we need it."

"Make that two." Colum held up a Land Rover fob. "Lucky for us Astrid didn't realize I had a spare set of keys in my night-stand drawer at the Claddagh. Since she hasn't bothered to conceal the Land Rover, no doubt expecting us to be either locked in a cell or trapped in the caves, we now have that vehicle at our disposal."

"And it's much faster than this one," Hunt said.

"She underestimated her enemy," Colum observed. "A mistake often made in battle."

"She miscalculated, for sure." Hunt was still studying the distant house. "But we should be wary of becoming complacent. She and Grendel are still dangerous, perhaps even more so given that Astrid has already made one foolish mistake. She will not want to make another."

"Which is why we should proceed as quickly as possible," Decker said. "The longer we sit idle, the greater likelihood that she will discover our presence."

"A valid observation." Hunt nodded to Colum, indicating that he should start up the driveway. "As quickly as you can, and let's keep our wits about us."

Colum moved forward and swung the steering wheel, bringing the car around onto the driveway and approaching the house.

As they entered the shadow of the building, Hunt spoke up.

"Pull up close to the Land Rover. Put us between it and the house."

"On it." Colum followed Hunt's directions and brought the car to a halt.

"Everyone out, quick as you can from the passenger side." Hunt was already exiting the car. "And stay low."

They piled out, using the car as a shield. Colum climbed from the driver's seat over to the passenger side and scooted out through the passenger door. Decker wondered if Astrid might be armed, and waited for the crack of a gunshot, but then remembered that they were in Ireland, not the United States. While it was not inconceivable that she might have a rifle or even a pistol, the chances were much lower. But this wasn't the main reason why Adam Hunt wanted them to climb out on that side of the vehicle. Once it became clear that no attack from the house was forthcoming, he motioned to Colum, who went to the back of the Land Rover and unlocked it, opening the rear hatch.

In most vehicles, the spare wheel would have been in the trunk under the floor, but on the Land Rover, the spare—in this case, the original rear wheel still bearing the punctures Harry Reardon's knife had inflicted a couple of days before—was attached to the outside of the rear door. This meant that the space underneath the trunk's floor could be used for something else. In this case, Decker saw, it had been used to conceal a veritable armory of weapons and other useful items. A field assault kit. Colum withdrew a couple of handguns, then gave one to Hunt, and offered the other to Rory.

"What am I going to do with that?" Rory hissed in a low voice.

"If you see Grendel, I suggest that you fire it." Colum pressed the gun into the man's hand.

"I'm an archaeologist, not a Navy seal," Rory said, holding the gun awkwardly in one hand.

"Hopefully, you won't need to use it." Colum winced and

moved the gun's barrel away from Hunt and Decker. "And for heaven's sake, don't point it at us."

"Sorry," Rory looked sheepish. "How is that stuff even in the trunk anyway? Were you expecting a war?"

"We equipped some of the CUSP cars to be armed response vehicles a few years ago. It's come in useful on more than one occasion."

"It's a good job Astrid didn't find that," Decker said.

"Yup." Colum delved back into the Land Rover's rear and pulled out a pair of Sig Sauer semi-automatic rifles with Surefire X300 tactical flashlights already mounted on the barrels. He handed one to Decker. "You look like you can handle this."

"I've been around the block," Decker said, taking the rifle.

Colum grunted and closed the trunk, but not before plucking a pair of two-way radios from the back. He returned to the group and handed one to Decker, then pushed the other one into his pocket. "Ready?"

Decker nodded. Hunt flashed an affirmative gesture with his free hand. Silent now, they moved around the vehicle, staying low, alert for any sign of attack. They mounted the house's front steps and hurried to the door. Here they regrouped.

Colum reached out and tried the door handle. "Locked."

"I wouldn't expect anything else," Hunt whispered.

"It won't be for long," Colum said. He stepped back and aimed the rifle at the door handle. "You guys might want to step to the side."

Hunt moved away from the door to the right. Decker steered Rory to the left. He raised his own gun in anticipation of entry.

"Here goes," Colum said. "If we haven't done so already, we're about to lose the element of surprise." Then he aimed the gun, his finger flexing on the trigger, and fired twice…

SIXTY-TWO

TWO BULLETS CRASHED into the door.

Splintered wood and shrapnel flew in all directions.

Decker turned away, covering his face. When he looked back there was a hole where the deadbolt securing the door had been. When Colum stepped forward and pushed upon it, the door swung easily inward.

"Knock, knock. Anyone home?" Colum muttered under his breath. He glanced toward the rest of the team. "This is our cue."

Decker kept his gun raised and moved toward the door with Colum beside him. He stepped into the house and scanned to the left for threats as Colum checked right.

They were standing in a wide entrance hall, with a grand bifurcated staircase that swept down from the floor above. Paintings hung on the walls; dark scenes of ancient battle contained by gold leafed frames. Hanging down through two floors, a glittering crystal chandelier. A checkerboard pattern of white tiles inset with smaller black diamonds made the space look even bigger than it actually was.

With the entrance swept for threats, Rory and Hunt joined their companions in the regal entryway, pistols raised.

"This is all very fancy-schmancy," Colum observed. "Not bad for a man-eating ogre, and his thousand-year-old mother."

"I guess that makes her a millennial," Rory quipped.

"Enough with the levity," Hunt's face was set in stone. "We have a job to do."

"Just letting off steam, boss," Colum said.

"There will be plenty of time for that later." Hunt was studying their surroundings. He looked up toward the second-floor landing as if he expected Grendel to come leaping over the railings toward them. "It's too quiet. I don't like it."

"If the fight won't come to us, we'll have to go to the fight," Colum said. He cast his eyes upward toward the second floor. "We need to search the house."

"It will go faster if we split up," Decker said. "This place looks huge."

"I don't like that idea," Hunt said. "A force divided is a force weakened."

"Decker's right." Colum grimaced. "I don't like it any more than you do, but Astrid and Grendel could be anywhere in this building, and we need to find them quickly or they may flee again."

"All right then," Hunt agreed grudgingly. He indicated Colum. "You take Rory, and I'll go with Decker."

"Sounds like a plan," Colum replied. "He pulled the walkie-talkie out of his pocket. "Let's keep in contact. If anyone finds Grendel and his mother, sound the alarm. Return here when you're done."

"Got it." Decker made sure his two-way radio was turned on. "You take the ground floor, we'll take the upper level."

Colum nodded and turned away, motioning for Rory to follow him. A moment later they disappeared through a door and into the spread of rooms beyond.

Decker glanced at Hunt. "Here we go then."

They mounted the stairs, guns at the ready, and then worked their way across the upper landing until they came to a long corridor with doors leading off on both sides. These were, presumably, the bedrooms. Decker stepped into the corridor, moving slowly, ready for trouble. At the first door they paused, standing one to each side, before Decker reached out and opened it.

He peered in.

The room was, indeed, a bedroom. A four-poster bed stood against one wall. A dresser with a tall mirror stood against the opposite wall. The furniture looked outdated. Antique. Other than that, the room was empty. They moved on to the next door and repeated the process. Again nothing. This they did—finding three more spacious bedrooms, and two bathrooms with claw foot tubs—until they reached the end of the corridor.

On the other side of the staircase, there was another identical corridor running in the opposite direction. As before, they went door to door, checking each room and finding them empty.

They returned to the head of the staircase. If Grendel and Astrid were in the house, they were not on the upper floor.

They started back down the staircase.

Decker keyed the two-way radio and spoke into it. "Upper floor is clear. Heading back to rendezvous point in entrance hall."

The radio hissed for a moment and then sprang to life in a squawk of static. "Roger that, John. Ground floor is secure. Returning now."

No sooner had Colum replied, then he and Rory appeared.

"The house is empty. I don't get it." Colum looked frustrated. "We know she came here, the Land Rover is parked outside."

"Maybe she had another vehicle and left again before we got here," Hunt said.

"Why would she go to the trouble of coming here, only to take a different vehicle and leave again?" Decker rubbed his chin thoughtfully. "She could have gone anywhere in the Land Rover. She didn't know it was being tracked."

"Maybe she figured it out," Rory said. "She's smart."

"She's still here," Decker said. "I can feel it."

"Where is she then?" Hunt asked.

"I don't know." Decker glanced around, convinced they must have overlooked something. At first, he didn't see anything, but then his eyes settled on a narrow door set into the side of the staircase. It was hard to spot, painted the same color as the woodwork on the stairs, but he knew instantly where it went. And then the empty house made sense. "The cellar."

"What?" Colum's gaze drifted to where Decker was looking. "My God, you're right. This house has a cellar."

"That's where they will be, I'll stake my life on it." Decker started toward the door. "Grendel has spent more than a thousand years living in darkness, why would he stop now."

"We're really going down there?" Rory said, a tremble in his voice.

"Yeah, I think we are." Decker reached out and gripped the door handle. The door swung back on well-oiled hinges. Beyond, he saw nothing but blackness.

Colum activated the flashlight on his gun and pointed it through the doorway. Decker followed suit. In the beam of their flashlights, they saw a set of wooden steps descending into a dank, cobweb infested cellar.

"This is just great," Rory said.

"Quit your grumbling," Colum replied, stepping past the door. He started down the stairs with Hunt at his rear.

"Maybe someone should stay up here and keep watch." Rory glanced back toward the front door, as if he wished he could head in that direction instead of down into the darkness.

"Just get in there," Decker pushed Rory along, and together they descended the stairs.

When they reached the bottom, they found themselves in a large underground space full of the discarded relics of a centuries old building. From somewhere to their left a small furry form scurried out of the glare of their lights. A big, fat rat.

Decker shuddered and moved off through the cellar, ducking in places to avoid low beams.

"They aren't down here either," Hunt said.

"Does that mean we can go back upstairs?" Rory asked, hopeful.

"I don't think so, not just yet." Decker was looking at an opening in the far wall, a jagged semicircular break in the brickwork supporting the house. "I know where Grendel and Astrid are. They're in that cave."

SIXTY-THREE

DECKER STOOD at the cave entrance and shined his light down into the murky darkness. "It makes sense that Astrid would have a house sitting on top of a cave system."

"Even before the Danes brought him to Ireland, Grendel was a cave dweller," Rory replied. The excitement of imparting knowledge had, it appeared, momentarily overcome his unease at being in the cellar. "In the original poem, he and his mother live in a labyrinth beneath a lake, surrounded by swamplands. Astrid's been searching for Grendel for centuries. She'd want him to feel at home when she found him."

"Enough talking," Hunt was growing impatient. "Grendel's down there, I know it. Let's go get him."

"Follow me. Keep close." Decker kept his gun raised and ducked into the cave. His flashlight beam cut through the darkness highlighting smooth stone walls, and a rocky floor. He wondered how long the tunnel was, but it was impossible to tell. All he saw ahead was swirling blackness beyond the scope of the light.

He moved forward with trepidation, aware that an attack could come at any time. He imagined Grendel rushing out of the darkness, teeth barred, oversized hands reaching out to rip him limb from limb. Decker shuddered and resisted the urge to turn back.

They walked on for several minutes, following the tunnel. Unlike the labyrinth under Clareconnell, this cave did not branch off or split, but was a straight shaft into Hades. Finally, the cave walls widened, and the sloping floor leveled off. Up ahead, a chamber came into view, a vast space that swallowed the flashlight beams.

Decker held up an arm, bringing the group to a stop. If Grendel and Astrid were going to be anywhere, it would be here. He motioned to Colum, silently instructing the man to keep his eyes peeled to the right as they approached the space. That done, he set off again, with Colum at his side, while the others followed to the rear. If they found Grendel, the rifles would be better protection than the smaller and less powerful handguns Rory and Hunt carried.

They were close to the end of the tunnel now. Up ahead, Decker could see an expanse of rocky boulder strewn ground stretching in all directions. Then, further afield, an arching wall of rock that stretched upward and out of sight. This was the back wall of the cavern. And crouched at its base, waiting for them, was Grendel…

SIXTY-FOUR

GRENDEL SHIELDED himself from Decker's flashlight beam and let out a mewling, angry hiss. Decker kept the gun aimed, his finger tensing on the trigger. To his side, he heard Colum draw in a sharp breath. For a moment, time stood still.

"What are you waiting for? Shoot it." Rory was peering over Decker's shoulders, his eyes wide with fear. "Quickly, before it attacks."

"I'm not shooting a defenseless creature," Decker replied, his eyes never straying from the beast. "Even if it is a monster."

Astrid's voice drifted from the darkness. "How very commendable of you." She moved out of the darkness. "I must say, I'm surprised to see you here. I thought I'd taken care of you in the caves."

"Sorry to disappoint you," Decker said.

"And you tracked me here, too." Astrid smiled, but there was no mirth to it. "How resourceful. Let me guess, the Land Rover."

Colum glared at her. "Did you really think we wouldn't have a tracker in that car?"

"Ah, of course. A regrettable oversight," Astrid replied. "Not that it matters. In fact, you've done me a favor."

"How's that?" Colum asked.

"I was just about to make something to eat. Grendel's hungry. How considerate of you to save me the trouble." The smile vanished from Astrid's face. She stepped forward, into the flashlight beam, shading Grendel from it with her body. She glanced backward at her son. "They are all yours."

Grendel's cowering hiss now turned into a bellow of starving rage. He shot forward, sidestepping his mother, and leapt at the clustered group of men.

"Shit." Colum raised his gun, trying to find Grendel in midair. His flashlight beam danced across the ceiling, momentarily illuminating the beast, before losing it again in the darkness.

"Back into the tunnel," Decker shouted, bringing his own gun to bear, but it was too late.

Grendel was already upon them. He landed between Colum and Decker, too close to engage with the rifles. His arm shot out, knocking Colum's gun away even as he tried to find enough space to discharge it. The weapon flew from Colum's grasp and clattered away into the darkness. Grendel let out a victorious shriek and took hold of the Irishman, hurled him into the cavern. Colum hung in the air for a moment, then smacked to the ground, rolled, and lay still.

Decker pushed Rory and Hunt further back into the tunnel and blocked them with his body. He managed to get off a shot as Grendel advanced upon him. The blast was deafening in the confined space. The bullet smashed home, a direct hit to Grendel's chest. The beast staggered backwards but appeared otherwise unhurt. There was, Decker noted with shock, not a trace of blood.

"That won't work with Grendel," Rory said, panicked. "The ancient text recounts that swords couldn't pierce his hide. That's why the Danes brought him here. They couldn't kill him."

Decker fired a second shot. Grendel staggered back again. Even if the bullets weren't doing any damage, they were at least keeping him at bay. He let loose with a third blast in quick succession. "You could've mentioned this before now."

"It didn't seem relevant," Rory said, waving the pistol in the general direction of the battle.

"Next time, tell me anyway." Decker squeezed off two more rounds. He could sense Hunt at his rear, silently evaluating the situation. He glanced toward Colum, twenty feet away in the cavern. He had moved. Decker hoped he wasn't dead. "Adam, I'll cover Grendel and keep him occupied. Go in there and get Colum back."

"On your mark," Hunt said.

Decker squeezed the trigger two more times. The rapid succession of bullets forced Grendel further backwards. The beast howled in anger and slapped at his chest even though the slugs could not penetrate. When he opened up a wide enough gap, Decker risked a glance backwards toward Hunt. "Go."

Hunt sidestepped Decker and sprinted into the cave, pistol at the ready.

"Don't touch him," Astrid screeched as Hunt approached Colum, who still lay helpless and unconscious on the ground. "He's for Grendel."

"You don't tell me what to do, bitch." Hunt aimed the pistol and fired.

Astrid, unlike her son, was not impervious to bullets. The 9mm shell tore through her right shoulder, the impact twisting her sideways. She let out a gasp of pain.

Grendel turned his attention from Decker toward Hunt. Anger flickered in his eyes. Then he barreled toward the American with a bloodcurdling roar.

SIXTY-FIVE

"LOOK OUT!" Decker shouted a frantic warning.

But Hunt had already seen the danger descending upon him. He fired the pistol twice in a vain attempt to fell the approaching beast, then gripped Colum by the collar and started dragging him back towards the cave entrance. The bullets slowed Grendel but otherwise did no harm. He swatted them away with an angry grunt and kept going.

Hunt was moving too slowly, Decker realized. Colum's limp body was acting like an anchor. Another second, and Grendel would have the helpless pair in its grasp. He pointed at Rory. "Stay there. Whatever you do, don't leave the tunnel."

"You can count on that," Rory said, holding the pistol out in front of him at arm's length with both hands.

Decker stepped back into the cave and aimed the rifle at the beast. He fired once, twice, three times. Grendel batted the bullets, but they did their job, arresting his forward motion, briefly. But it was enough time for Decker to reach Hunt and assist him. Together they dragged Colum back into the tunnel.

"Is he alive?" Decker asked, positioning himself between the cavern and the rest of the group.

"Yes, he's breathing." Hunt was kneeling over Colum.

"The two of you will need to carry him," Decker said. "I'll provide cover." He wondered how many rounds the gun held. It couldn't be more than twenty, and he'd fired at least eight times already, maybe more. In the heat of the moment, he hadn't kept count. Almost half the ammunition was gone. It wouldn't take long to deplete the rest. Colum's gun was still in the cavern, but there was no way Decker would be able to reach it. Grendel was already at the tunnel entrance. His lips curled back in a vicious snarl.

Behind him, holding a hand to her ruined shoulder in an attempt to staunch the blood, was Astrid. Decker was under no illusion that the wound would kill her. She hadn't survived a thousand years only to be felled by one small bullet. He wondered what would've happened if Hunt had managed a kill shot, a bullet to the head or heart. Would that be enough to vanquish her? He wasn't sure. Astrid looked human, but underneath lurked a monster as dark and twisted as Grendel himself. Whatever supernatural powers had kept the pair alive for so long tipped the scales in their favor. But that was all the time Decker got to ponder the subject because Grendel was approaching now, entering the tunnel, and advancing with slow, measured steps.

They were trapped, and he knew it.

Even if Decker and the others were able to retreat back to the cellar, they would never make it up the stairs before Grendel killed them. Especially with Colum out of action and the dead weight.

The situation felt hopeless.

Decker aimed the gun and fired another round. It smacked into the approaching beast but as expected, did no damage.

Decker let out a frustrated grunt. Another bullet gone. And when the rest of them ran out, they would be defenseless. He aimed the rifle to squeeze off one more shot but then thought better of it. Grendel was having fun stalking them, in no hurry to finish the job. The beast kept his distance, close enough that he could attack should he wish, but far enough away to savor their fear. Until Grendel actually charged, there was no point in wasting more ammunition. He raised the gun, adjusting his grip, ready for Grendel's final assault. As he did so, the beam from the flashlight on the barrel danced momentarily across the cave ceiling, and in that brief instant, Decker saw something.

A fissure in the rock.

A deep fault line that ran across the tunnel's ceiling a few feet ahead of the approaching beast.

This gave Decker an idea.

Except that Grendel had gotten bored stalking them. Or maybe he'd read Decker's mind. Either way, he let out a deafening roar and lumbered forward towards them.

Decker froze, the gun still lifted toward the ceiling.

Hunt, a few steps ahead of Decker in the tunnel, let out an exasperated gasp. "What are you waiting for, man? Shoot at the damn thing."

"Shooting Grendel won't do any good," Decker barked, flexing a finger on the trigger of the upward aimed gun. "I know what I'm doing."

"Well, for heaven's sake, do it then."

"I hope this works," Decker said and pulled the trigger several times in rapid succession.

The tunnel exploded in a cacophony of booming sound. The gun's muzzle flashes lit Grendel in a staccato dance that gave him the appearance of a monster in some old 1940s B-movie.

Then the world collapsed around them.

With a mighty groan, the fissure in the ceiling widened as the bullets slammed into it. A huge slab of rock slipped out of place. It held for a second, fighting gravity, and then fell in Grendel's path.

The beast jumped back out of the way with an alarmed squeal.

A shudder ran through the tunnel.

Cracks weaved out across the ceiling to the accompaniment of sharp snapping sounds.

More rocks rained down.

Decker lowered the gun and turned, realizing that his plan may have been too successful. The roof was more fragile than he'd anticipated. Not only would it bury Grendel, but it would probably bury them too.

"We need to get out of here right now," Decker said, slipping Colum's limp arm around his shoulders, relieving Rory, who was struggling under the weight. Together they half carried, half dragged, Colum back toward the cellar, while behind them, Grendel beaten back by falling rocks, howled in frustration.

They reached the cellar and tumbled forward out of the tunnel. And not a moment too soon. The sharp popping sounds that signaled fresh cracks in the roof had stopped now. For one second, calm descended. Decker turned and looked back down the tunnel to see Grendel pulling himself over a pile of fallen rock. Their eyes met briefly. Beast and man. Hunter and Hunted.

And then the ceiling crashed down.

A billowing cloud of dust belched from the tunnel, followed by a hailstorm of small rocks that clattered around them. Decker turned away, covering his mouth, and waited for the air to clear. When he looked back, the tunnel was gone. All that remained was a solid wall of rubble.

Decker dropped his head, exhausted.

From behind him, a voice piped up. "Well that's just great; I missed all the fun."

Decker looked around to see Colum standing under his own steam. He cradled one arm, and he was bleeding from a gash on his forehead, but even so, there was a twinkle in his eye.

"It's okay," Decker said with a grin. "We handled it just fine without you."

The smile widened on Colum's face. "I knew that you would."

Rory watched the back-and-forth with pursed lips. Then he

spoke up. "If it's all the same with you guys, I'd really like to get out of here now. This action hero stuff really is not my forte."

"That sounds like a splendid idea," Colum said. He glanced at his watch. "If we hurry, I can get back to the Claddagh for a nice big Irish breakfast before they close . . ."

EPILOGUE

FOUR DAYS LATER

THEY SAT around a table at the Claddagh Arms, having been drawn together by Adam Hunt for a debriefing. Colum was making the most of the meeting and diving into an Irish breakfast, complete with the puddings he liked so much, even though it was early in the afternoon. It was, apparently, never too late for sausages and a fried egg. Decker couldn't help wondering how the ex-ranger had kept so fit given his proclivity for fried food. He watched Colum use the side of his fork to break the food up, his other arm in a sling, thanks to his run in days before with Grendel. The arm was not broken, he merely suffered a dislocated shoulder, but he would be incapacitated for several more days.

Adam Hunt waited until Harry had brought them pints of beer before commencing the meeting. "I just want to congratulate everyone on a job well done," he said, looking around the group. "Astrid and Grendel have been successfully extracted from the cave under her house and are, as I speak, on their way to a more secure location."

"You mean the Zoo." Rory picked up his pint and sipped it.

"I'll feel better once we get word that they've been processed and safely locked up."

"As will I," Hunt said.

"What's the Zoo?" Decker asked. He felt that Hunt was holding back a great deal of information and wondered when he would be fully trusted with CUSP's secrets.

"It's where we put the more troublesome specimens if we capture them alive," Colum said looking up from his food. "I've only been there a couple of times but man, did it give me the creeps."

"I think that's enough talk of the Zoo. Do remember that we are not in a secure location." If Hunt was mad at some perceived breach of protocol, he kept his voice on an even keel regardless. "Suffice it to say the ghost team did a good job. The Irish authorities never even knew they were there."

"Those guys are tough." Colum shook his head. "I don't envy them their job. I wouldn't want to do it."

"Ghost team?" Again, Decker felt like he was playing catch-up.

Hunt leaned close. "Specialists in transferring dangerous subjects. They also handle our on-site cleanup operations. By now, there will be no evidence that anything untoward ever occurred at that house."

"Speaking of which, there's one thing I don't get," Decker said. "We used weapons from the back of the Land Rover to mount our offensive on Astrid and Grendel in that cave under the house. Yet the day before when we went up to the caves under the monastery you brought along a crowbar."

"And?"

"We rode up to the monastery in the Land Rover. If there was an entire arsenal of weapons and other useful items stowed under the trunk floor, why did we bother with a crowbar? You suspected that Grendel may not be a pile of bones, so why risk running into him with such a paltry weapon when better ones were at hand?"

"I was wondering when someone would bring that up." A faint smile touched Hunt's lips. "The answer is simple. I didn't trust Astrid. Her explanation regarding being lost in the caves when we first arrived did not add up. She claimed that she became disoriented looking for a way to reach Robert after he fell, and yet a more logical approach would've been to return to the surface and fetch help. Given my doubts about her truthfulness, I was loath to provide her with any kind of weapon that she might have been able to use against us. As you will recall, I did my best to dissuade her from accompanying us up to the ruins that night, but she insisted on going."

"We only succeeded in containing her and Grendel because she didn't know about the armory concealed in the Land Rover's trunk," Colum said. "If Adam had tipped our hand by making her aware of those weapons it would've been a very different outcome."

"You risked our lives on a hunch." Decker wasn't sure if he should be impressed or angry.

"It was my call to make," Hunt said. "Bear in mind, I was not sure that Grendel was still alive. Common sense would point to the contrary. I felt that Astrid was being deceitful although I didn't know why, therefore she was the known threat at the time. It was a calculated gamble. You would have done the same if you were in charge, I'm sure."

Decker nodded. He'd followed his gut many times and had been correct more often than not. There was more he wanted to ask, but at that moment the pub's front door opened and Sean entered.

He nodded a quick greeting to Harry, who was wiping glasses with a cloth and putting them on a shelf behind the bar. Then he Made a beeline for their table. "I was hoping I'd find you guys here. I wanted to drop in and say goodbye."

"Are you going somewhere?" Colum asked. "Because I'm sure as hell not while Harry's still making these delicious breakfasts. I don't know why, but the food tastes so much better here than in the city."

"Ignore him," Hunt said. "He's taking painkillers for that arm of his, and I think it's clouding his mind."

"I am going somewhere," Sean replied. He glanced toward Colum. "Your neck of the woods actually."

"Dublin?" Colum pushed his empty plate away. "Are you having yourself a vacation?"

"Not quite. I'm taking Ellen and were getting out of here, just as soon as we've buried Craig. The diocese is sending a new priest, and I've given the village one of my fields to turn into a cemetery. The neighbor next door is buying the rest of the farm. After all that has happened, it's time to make a fresh start far from here."

"You and Ellen are a couple now?" Colum looked surprised. "That was quick."

"I'd not say we're a couple just yet, but we will be. Craig was my best friend, but I've known Ellen just as long. He'd be happy that the two people who meant the most to him are together. Of course, I'd rather that Craig was…"

"We understand." Hunt stood and held his hand out to Sean. "Good luck in your new life."

"Thanks." Sean took the hand and shook it. He turned to leave but when he was halfway across the room he stopped and turned back to the group. "I just need to know one thing."

"What?" Hunt asked.

"Grendel and Astrid. They're well and truly taken care of right? They won't ever be able to hurt anyone again?"

"You have my word," Hunt replied.

Sean nodded, then he continued on his way, the pub door closing behind him as he left.

The group sat in silence for a moment, each lost in their own thoughts, and then Colum spoke up. "So, boss, what's next? I'm thinking the four of us should go explore some strange happenings in the South of France, or maybe the Bahamas. I could go for a margarita or two in between chasing monsters."

"Sounds good to me," Rory said with a smile.

"Sorry to disappoint you, boys," Hunt said. "But I'm not sure I can swing that one. Rory and I are off back to the States first thing in the morning. I have a stack of research for our resident archaeologist."

"Perfect." Rory didn't look pleased. "I can hardly wait."

"What about the newbie?" Colum asked, nodding toward Decker. "You not taking him with you?"

"Funny you should ask that. There's a little situation I need the pair of you to handle, and I'm afraid it's quite urgent. I have been made aware of a rather nasty murderer on the loose. You're on the first flight out of Dublin tomorrow, bound for London."

"London?" Decker was surprised.

"Wouldn't Scotland Yard be better at catching a murderer?" Colum asked. "It's not really our job."

"It is this time," Hunt pulled a manila envelope from a satchel leaning against the leg of his chair. He threw it down on the table.

Decker looked down at the folder, then glanced up in surprise. "You can't be serious."

"I'm very serious," Hunt replied.

Decker's eyes fell to the folder again, just to make sure he'd read it right the first time. There, written on the front in bold black capitals, a name he never thought he'd see on an active case file.

Jack the Ripper.

THE NEXT BOOK IN THE JOHN DECKER SERIES

Whitechapel Rising

An impossible killer stalks the streets of London.

Jack the Ripper faded into history over a century ago, his identity lost to the ages. Until a work crew restoring a Mayfair home make a shocking find. A secret basement room walled up since Victorian times. The Whitechapel murderer's lair. And inside, a corpse that has waited in silent darkness for over a hundred years. But it won't stay that way...

Within hours of the room's discovery, the body goes missing, and the murders begin anew.

With a violent killer on the loose and the body count rising, John Decker, still new to CUSP, is sent to England, along with seasoned operative Colum O'Shea. Their mission—to stop a ruthless monster from obtaining the one thing that will allow him to escape forever.

As the city huddles in fear and the terror mounts, Decker finds himself in a race against time to catch a hellish fiend smarter than any he has ever faced. Because if he doesn't, the next death might hit a little too close to home.

ABOUT THE AUTHOR

Anthony M. Strong is a British-born writer living and working in the United States. He is the author of the popular John Decker series of supernatural adventure thrillers.

Anthony has worked as a graphic designer, newspaper writer, artist, and actor. When he was a young boy, he dreamed of becoming an Egyptologist and spent hours reading about pyramids and tombs. Until he discovered dinosaurs and decided to be a paleontologist instead. Neither career panned out, but he was left with a fascination for monsters and archaeology that serve him well in the John Decker books.

Anthony has traveled extensively across Europe and the United States, and weaves his love of travel into his novels, setting them both close to home and in far-off places.

Anthony currently resides most of the year on Florida's Space Coast where he can watch rockets launch from his balcony, and part of the year on an island in Maine, with his wife Sonya, and two furry bosses, Izzie and Hayden.

Connect with Anthony, find out about new releases, and get free books at www.anthonymstrong.com

Printed in Great Britain
by Amazon

27587625R00149